"I don't believe I have ever seen so many women gathered in one place before. There must be thousands."

Tess tensed. "Wait. How will you find us again if we go inside without you?"

"I could probably spot you in the crowd by your pr… By your hair," Michael said.

"You were going to say pretty, weren't you?" She smiled, amused by the way his cheeks grew more ruddy.

"It would be wrong of me to mention such things, Miss Clark."

That made her laugh softly. "But I would find it delightful if you did. Does that embarrass you, Michael?"

"Of course not."

He brought the buggy to a halt, then quickly helped her alight. "I'll find you."

She knew that her eyes must be twinkling, because she was keenly amused when she shouted back, "And how will you do *that*, sir?"

Michael paused just long enough to lean down from his perch. "By your beautiful, dark red hair." Then he flicked the reins and the horse took off.

Books by Valerie Hansen

Love Inspired Historical

Frontier Courtship
Wilderness Courtship
High Plains Bride
The Doctor's
 Newfound Family
Rescuing the Heiress

Love Inspired

*The Perfect Couple
*Second Chances
*Love One Another
*Blessings of the Heart
*Samantha's Gift
*Everlasting Love
The Hamilton Heir
*A Treasure of the Heart
Healing the Boss's Heart

Love Inspired Suspense

*Her Brother's Keeper
*Out of the Depths
Deadly Payoff
*Shadow of Turning
Hidden in the Wall
*Nowhere to Run
*No Alibi
My Deadly Valentine
*"Dangerous Admirer"

*Serenity, Arkansas

VALERIE HANSEN

was thirty when she awoke to the presence of the Lord in her life and turned to Jesus. In the years that followed she worked with young children, both in church and secular environments. She also raised a family of her own and played foster mother to a wide assortment of furred and feathered critters.

Married to her high school sweetheart since age seventeen, she now lives in an old farmhouse she and her husband renovated with their own hands. She loves to hike the wooded hills behind the house and reflect on the marvelous turn her life has taken. Not only is she privileged to reside among the loving, accepting folks in the breathtakingly beautiful Ozark mountains of Arkansas, she also gets to share her personal faith by telling the stories of her heart for all of Steeple Hill's Love Inspired lines.

Life doesn't get much better than that!

RESCUING THE
Heiress

VALERIE HANSEN

Steeple
Hill®

Published by Steeple Hill Books™

STEEPLE HILL BOOKS

Steeple
Hill®

Recycling programs
for this product may
not exist in your area.

ISBN-13: 978-0-373-82855-5

RESCUING THE HEIRESS

www.SteepleHill.com

Printed in U.S.A.

Though I walk in the midst of trouble,
you preserve my life…with your
right hand you save me, Lord.
—*Psalms* 138:7

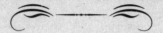

My husband was a firefighter, my son
still is and my daughter also volunteered
before she went into nursing.

The men and women in the fire service put
their whole hearts into their work and no amount of
praise or thanks for their efforts will ever be enough.

Chapter One

1906, San Francisco

"We can't ask Michael to do it. What would your father say if he found out?"

Tess Clark squared her shoulders, lifted her chin and smiled at the personal maid who had also become her friend and confidante. "Of course we can, Annie dear. Father would much rather we be escorted to the meeting by a gentleman than venture out unaccompanied, especially after dark. Besides, your mother's planning to attend, isn't she?"

"She said she might. But she lives down by the pavilion. She's used to being out and about in that neighborhood after dark." The slim young woman shivered. "It's no place for a society girl like you."

"Humph." Tess shook her head, making her dainty pearl earbobs swing. "Just because my family lives on Nob Hill doesn't mean I'm that different from other people. I want to support the cause of women's rights as much as you do." She pressed her lips into a thin line. "Maybe more so."

"But…"

Adamant, Tess stood firm. "No arguments. We're going to the meeting. I intend to hear Maud Younger speak before she goes back to New York, and we may never have a better opportunity."

"You're not afraid of what your father will do when he finds out?"

"I didn't say that," Tess admitted wryly. "Father can be very forceful at times. He'd certainly be irate if we made the journey alone. That's why we need a strapping escort like Michael Mahoney."

Annie covered her mouth with her hand and snickered. "And handsome, too."

Tess couldn't argue. She'd have had to be wearing blinders to have missed noticing how the family cook's son had matured, especially since he'd reached his mid-twenties. Truth to tell, Tess had done more than notice. She had dreamed of what her life might be like if she were a mere domestic like Annie rather than the daughter of wealthy banker Gerald Bell Clark. She might sometimes choose to view herself as a middle-class resident of the City by the Bay but that didn't mean she would be accepted as such by anyone who knew who she really was.

"I just had a thought," Tess said, eyeing her boon companion and beginning to smile. "I think it would be wise if we both attend the lecture incognito. I still have a few of my mother's old hats and wraps. It'll be like playing dress-up when we were children."

Annie rolled her blue eyes, eyes that matched Tess's as if they were trueborn sisters. "To listen to your papa talk, you'd think we were still babes instead of eighteen. Why, we're nearly old maids."

That made Tess laugh. "Hardly, dear. But I do see your point. Papa probably sees us as children because he's so prone to dwell on the past. He never talks about it but I don't think he's ever truly recovered from Mama's passing."

"I miss her, too," Annie said. "She was a lovely lady."

"And one who would want to march right along with us, arm in arm, if she were still alive," Tess said with conviction.

"March? Oh, dear. We aren't going to have to do that, are we? I mean, what will people say if we're seen as part of an unruly mob? Susan B. Anthony was arrested!"

"And she stood up for her rights just the same," Tess said with a lift of her chin. "According to the literature I've read, she never has paid the fines the courts levied."

"That's all well and good for a crusader like her. What about me? If your father finds out I went with you, he might fire me. You know my mother can't do enough sewing and mending to support me and herself. She barely gets by with what I manage to add to her income. If I lost this job…"

"You won't," Tess assured her.

"You can't be sure of that."

"I know that my father is a fair man. And he does love me—in his own way—so he'll listen if I find it necessary to defend you. I think sometimes that he's afraid to show much affection, perhaps because of Mama."

"You do resemble her. Same dark red hair, same sky-blue eyes, fair skin and sweet smile."

Tess began to blush. "Thank you. I always thought she was beautiful."

"So are you," Annie insisted. "The only real difference I can see is that you're so terribly stubborn and willful."

"That I get from my father," Tess said with a quiet chuckle, "and glad of it. Otherwise, how could I possibly hope to stand up to him, express my wishes and actually prevail?"

"When have you done that?"

"Well…" Tess's cheeks warmed even more. "I shall. Someday. When I have a cause, a reason that I feel warrants such boldness."

"Like woman suffrage, you mean?"

Tess sobered. "Yes. That's exactly what I mean. Now, go find Michael and tell him what we need. Look in the kitchen. It's Friday so he should be visiting his mother."

"You keep track of his schedule?"

"Of course not. I just happened to remember that he has every other Friday afternoon free, that's all, and I don't believe I noticed him being here last week." She looked away, taking a moment to compose herself and hoping Annie wouldn't press her for a better explanation.

"Come with me?"

Tess arched a slim eyebrow. "You're not afraid of him, are you?"

"No, I just get this funny, fluttery feeling in my stomach when I see him and I can hardly speak, let alone be convincing. It's as if my tongue is tied."

Unfortunately, Tess knew *exactly* what Annie meant. Between the mischievous twinkle in the man's dark eyes and his hint of an Irish brogue, he was truly captivating. "All right. We'll both go. He might be more likely to agree to accompany us if I asked him."

"Of course. He won't want to jeopardize his mother's job by refusing."

It bothered Tess to hear that rationale. She had hoped to persuade the attractive, twenty-four-year-old fireman to do her bidding by simply appealing to his gallantry. The suggestion that her family's importance, both at home on the Clark estate and in the city proper, might be a stronger influence was disheartening.

It was also true.

Michael Mahoney had come straight from work, shedding his brass-buttoned, dark wool uniform jacket and leather-beaked cap as soon as he entered the overly warm kitchen of the Clark estate.

He gave his mother a peck on the cheek, took a deep breath and sighed loudly for her benefit. "Mmm, something smells heavenly."

Clearly pleased, Mary grinned and chuckled. "Of course it does."

"Will you be wanting more apples peeled?" he asked, starting to turn back his shirt cuffs while eyeing a sugar-and-cinnamon-topped bowl of already prepared fruit. "I'll be glad to help, especially if I get to taste one of those pies you're making." He pulled a stool up to the table and sat down.

Hands dusted with flour, Mary was rolling circles of crust at the opposite end of the work-worn oak surface. "That's no job for an important man like you, Michael." She used the back of her wrist to brush a wispy curl away from her damp forehead. "You have a career now. You don't need to be helpin' me."

"Clark should have hired you a kitchen maid long ago," Michael said flatly. "With all his money you'd think he'd be glad to lighten your burdens."

"I've had a few girls here. None lasted. They were too lazy. 'Twas easier for me to just jump in and do their chores than to wait."

"Still, I think I should have a talk with him."

"Don't you dare. I'd be mortified."

"Why?"

"Because Mr. Clark is a good man and a fine boss. I wouldn't want him thinkin' I wasn't grateful. He gave me a raise in salary you know."

"Over a year ago or longer. If Mrs. Clark was still in the household you'd have gotten more than just the one."

"I know. She was such a darling girl, poor thing.

The mister's not been the same since she passed." Mary sighed deeply, noisily. "I know how he feels. Sometimes it seems like your da will walk in the door one day and greet me the way he did for so many wonderful years."

Michael chose not to respond. His father had been lost at sea while working as a seaman almost ten years ago, and before that had only come home on rare occasions. If they hadn't had a fading photograph of the man, Michael wondered if he'd have been able to picture him at all.

"It's been a long time," he said. "You're still a comely woman. Why not set your cap for a man who can take care of you?"

"Now, why would I be wantin' to do that when my lovin' son is goin' to look after me in me old age?"

Chuckling, Michael nodded. "All right. You've made your point. And I will, you know. I just have to work my way up in the department until I'm making enough money to feed us both and qualify for family housing." He laughed more. "I don't suppose you'd be wantin' to live in the station house with all those rowdy boys and me."

"Might remind me of my brothers back in Eire, but, no, I have a nice room here. I'll wait till you're better set before I make my home with you."

He reached to steal a slice of cinnamon-flecked apple from the bowl and was rewarded by her "Tsk-tsk" and a playful swat in his direction.

"I always knew you were a wise woman," he said, popping the tangy bit into his mouth.

"And don't you be forgettin' it," Mary warned.

From the doorway came a softly spoken, "Forget what?"

Michael's head snapped around and he jumped to his feet. He knew that voice well, yet hearing it never ceased to give him a jolt. Whether it was a sense of joy or of tension, he had not been able to decide.

Licking his lips and dusting sugar granules off his hands, he nodded politely. "Miss Tess. Miss Annie. Good afternoon."

Annie giggled and followed Tess into the warm kitchen.

"Umm. That bread baking smells wonderful. I can hardly wait to butter a slab," Tess said.

Mary gave a slight curtsy and wiped her floury hands on her apron as she eyed the imposing gas stove. "Thank you, miss. It should be ready soon."

"Then perhaps we'll wait." Tess looked to Michael and gave him a slight smile. "How have you been?"

"Fine, thank you. I just dropped in to pay a call on my mother."

"As you should. Your employment is progressing satisfactorily, I presume?"

"Yes. I'm next in line to be promoted to captain of my fire company."

"How impressive. I wish you well."

He'd been studying Tess as she spoke and sensed that there was more on her mind than mere polite formalities. She and Annie had both been acting unduly uneasy, paying him close attention and fidgeting more than was normal for either of them.

"Thank you," Michael said with a lopsided, knowing smile. "Why am I getting the impression that you ladies have something else to say?"

"Perhaps because we do," Tess said. He saw her tighten the clasp of her hands at her waist and noticed that she was worrying a lace-edged handkerchief in her slim fingers.

"And what would that be?"

"I—we—are in sore need of an escort this evening and we were wondering if you would be so kind."

"An escort?" Michael's brow knit. "Don't you have a beau who can provide that service?"

Tess's cheeks flamed but she held her ground. "At the moment, sadly, no. However, Annie and I would be honored if you could find the time to accompany us. We can use one of father's carriages if you like."

His dark eyebrows arched. "Oh? And where would we be going?"

"Mechanics' Pavilion. There's going to be—"

"Whoa. I know what's going on there tonight. I won't be a party to your participation in such a folly."

"I beg your pardon?"

Well, now I've ruffled her feathers, Michael concluded, seeing her eyes widen and hearing the rancor in her tone. Nevertheless, he knew he was right. "The pardon you should be beggin' is your father's," he said flatly. "Mr. Clark has a reputation to maintain, for himself and for his bank. You can't be keepin' company with the likes of those crazy women."

"I can and I will," Tess insisted. "If you won't escort us, then we'll go alone."

His jaw gaped for a moment before he snapped it shut. "I almost believe you."

"You'd best do so, sir, because I mean every word."

Looking to his mother, Michael saw her struggling to subdue a smirk. That was a fine kettle of fish. His own ma was evidently siding with the younger women. What was this world coming to? Didn't they know their place? Hadn't men been taking good care of women like them for untold generations?

Sure there was the problem of widows and orphans, but there were benevolent societies to provide for those needs. The last thing San Francisco—or the entire nation—needed was to give women a say in politics. No telling where a mistake like that would eventually lead.

"I can't understand why you feel so strongly about this, Miss Tess. I've known you ever since my mother came to work here and I've never noticed such unreasonableness."

"It isn't unreasonable to want to hear the facts explained by one of the movement's leaders," Tess said.

Seeing the jut of her chin and the rigidity of her spine, he was convinced that she was serious so he tried another approach. "It could be dangerous. There have been riots as a result of such rabble-rousing."

"All the more reason why you should be delighted to look after us," she countered. "Well?"

Michael felt as stuck as a loaded freight wagon bogged down and sinking in quicksand. Slowly shaking his head, he nevertheless capitulated. "All right. I'm not scheduled to work tonight. If there are no fire alarms between now and then, I'll take you. What time do you want to leave?"

"The meeting commences at eight," Tess said. "I assume that's so wives and mothers will not have to neglect their families in order to attend. You may call for us at half past seven. I'll have the carriage ready."

With that she grabbed Annie's hand and quickly led her out of the room, their long, plaited skirts swishing around their ankles as they went.

Michael sank back onto the stool. When he glanced at his mother he noted that she was grinning from ear to ear.

"Well, well, if I hadn't seen it with me own eyes I'd not have believed it," Mary drawled. "My full-grown son was just steamrolled by a slip of a girl. 'Twas quite a sight."

"That it was," Michael said. "I can hardly believe it myself. What's happened to Tess? She used to be so levelheaded and obedient."

"You think she's not being sensible? Ha! If you ask me, she and others like her are going to come to the rescue of this wicked world. Imagine how those crooked politicians will squirm when they can't rely only on the good old boys who've been keeping them in office in spite of their evil shenanigans."

"Ma! Watch yourself. If Mr. Clark was to overhear you, he might think you were responsible for Tess's crazy notions."

"More likely that girl's responsible for waking me up," his mother replied. "If I didn't have so many chores tonight, I might just be tempted to go listen to Miss Younger, too."

Tess had raided the attic with Annie and they had both come away with elaborately decorated dark hats and veils.

Annie's was silk with the brim rolled to one side and the crown bedecked with silk and muslin cup roses and a taffeta bow.

Tess chose the one she had always loved seeing her mother wear. It had two sweeping ostrich plumes anchored in a rosette of shiny black taffeta centered with a large jet ornament. That pin had been a gift from her father to her mother and Mama had always adored it.

Their shirtwaist blouses and lightweight, plaited skirts were their own but they had covered them with heavy wool coats. Tess's reached below her ankles. Annie's brushed the floor.

"I'm too short," the girl complained, lifting the hem. "I'll get it all dusty."

"Better dust than mud," Tess countered. "Just be thankful it isn't as wet out there as it usually is in the spring."

She glanced from the second-floor window of her bedroom where they were finishing their preparations. The garden below was bathed in a light mist, and beyond toward the Pacific, clouds lay low, obscuring the moon and much of the landscape, including the lights of the parts of the city nearest the shore.

"Hopefully it won't rain later tonight," Tess said. "Looks like the fog is going to be bad though."

"I know. Maybe we shouldn't go out."

"Nonsense. Did you order my mare harnessed to the buggy and tell them when to bring it around, as we'd planned?"

"Yes. But I don't know that we'll have a driver. The last I saw of Michael he was still with Mary. I thought surely he'd want to go home and change if he truly intended to take us."

"I suspect he was wishing he'd be called back to work so he wouldn't have to keep that promise," Tess said. "I sincerely hope he doesn't spend the entire evening lecturing us on the proper place of women in the home."

Annie grinned. "He can't really do that unless he goes inside and listens to Miss Younger."

"Which is highly unlikely," Tess added. "Wasn't he funny when he got so uppity? Imagine thinking he can tell us what to do."

"He sounded like your father may when he finds out what we've been up to tonight." Annie was shivering in spite of the warmth of her wool coat. "I'm not looking forward to that."

"Nor am I," Tess replied with a slight nod, "but I truly

feel that this is a cause worth investigating. It's not as if you and I were planning to officially join the movement or anything like that. We're just curious. Think of it as a lark."

"Michael surely doesn't see it that way."

"No." Tess sobered. "But his opinion isn't our concern. As long as he lives up to his promise we'll have no trouble."

"I wish we'd asked someone else to escort us."

"I don't," Tess replied candidly. Truth to tell, she was looking forward to being driven into the heart of the city by the handsome fireman almost as much as she was looking forward to hearing the suffragette lecture.

She began to smile, then grin. There weren't many socially acceptable ways she could spend time with the cook's son. Not that she'd ever admit she was looking for any. Perish the thought. But this adventure would be fun. And perhaps in the long run, one more man would begin to understand why so many women were banding together to demand emancipation.

Annie's squeal startled her from her reverie. "The buggy's here!" She grabbed her hat to help hold it in place as she added another long pin. "It's time to go."

"All right, all right. Keep your voice down or Father will hear."

"Sorry." Annie pressed the fingertips of one hand to her lips while continuing to steady the large hat with her other. "Did you leave a note?"

"Yes," Tess whispered. "And I sincerely hope Father

doesn't find reason to miss us and read it." She reached for the other young woman's gloved hand. "Come on. Our carriage awaits."

Chapter Two

Here they come, Michael thought. *Or do they?* He shook his head in disbelief. Except for the lightness of their steps, the approaching pair resembled stodgy matrons rather than the lithe, lovely young women he had expected. If this was their idea of a joke he was not amused.

While a groom steadied the horse, Michael circled the cabriolet to assist them. Frowning, he offered his hand.

"Good evening, Mr. Mahoney," Tess said, placing her small, gloved fingers in his and raising her hem just enough to place her dainty foot on the step leading to the rear seat.

"It'll be good only if your father doesn't find out what you're up to," Michael countered. "I can't believe you convinced me to be a party to this."

Stepping aboard, she laughed softly, her eyes twinkling behind the thin veil that she'd arranged to cover her face. "Neither can I."

"You two look like you're going to a funeral," he said with disdain. "I just hope it isn't mine."

Tess merely laughed. Michael was too troubled to comment further. Instead, he helped Annie up the same step, then vaulted easily into the driver's seat. "Ready?"

"Ready," they said in unison, sounding like two happy children headed for a romp in Golden Gate Park on a sunny afternoon.

Their carefree attitude irritated Michael. He'd spent enough time in the seamier parts of San Francisco to know that his chore of protecting these foolish young women might prove harder than either of them imagined. Yes, the city was more civilized than it had been right after the gold rush, but there were still plenty of ne'er-do-wells, drunks and just plain crooks out and about, especially after dark.

His fondest hope was that the crowd of women at Mechanics' Pavilion would act as an adequate buffer to help safeguard his charges. He couldn't hold off a mob single-handed, not even if he were armed, which he was not.

An aroma of salt water and rotting refuse from down by the wharves was borne on the fog, although it didn't seem quite as offensive as usual, probably because the evening was quite cool and there was no onshore wind to carry as much of the odor inland.

Michael flicked the reins lightly to encourage the horse to trot after he turned onto Powell Street. Driving over the cobblestones with the metal-rimmed carriage wheels gave their passage a rough, staccato cadence, although there was so much other traffic on the wide boulevard the sounds melded into a clatter that made it hard to differentiate one noise from the others.

Teamsters yelled at their teams, whipping the poor beasts to force them to haul overfilled wagons up the steep streets from the wharves. A herd of cattle was evidently being driven up Market Street because their combined bellowing and shouts of the drovers working them could be heard blocks away.

Add to that the occasional echoing pistol shot, probably coming from the seamier areas of the city, and Michael was decidedly uneasy. The sooner they reached the pavilion and he got these two innocents settled inside the hall, the happier he'd be.

A giggle came from behind him, tickling the fine hairs at the nape of his neck. It was Tess. Of course it was. Annie might be accompanying her but this so-called adventure had most certainly originated in Tess's active mind.

He glanced over his shoulder. "What's so funny?"

"Nothing," Tess replied, her voice still tinged with humor. "I was just thinking of how much more enjoyable this jaunt would be if we'd taken Papa's new motorcar."

"You'd need a different driver if you had," Michael told her flatly. "I've plenty of experience handling the lines but never an automobile."

"You drive them with a wheel or a steering lever, not

reins," Tess teased. "Everybody knows that. Papa says the time will come when horses are unnecessary."

"I doubt that. Those machines will never catch on. Too noisy and complicated. Besides, you'd spend all your spare time stopping at pharmacies to buy jugs of fuel. Imagine the inconvenience."

"No more so than having to feed and water horses," she countered. "You should know all about that. Those fire horses you care for are beautiful animals. When they race through the streets as a team it's a thrilling sight."

"How would you know?"

She tittered behind her gloved hand. "I have seen them in action many times. And you driving them, if you must know."

"Have you, now? That's a bit of a surprise." When he turned slightly farther and smiled at her, he saw her gather herself and raise her chin.

"I can't understand why it should be. Station #4 is not too far from Father's bank and it is impossible to ignore that noisy, clanging bell and that steaming engine racing through the streets at such reckless speeds."

"It's only reckless if unheeding pedestrians step in front of us. The bell is meant to be enough warning for any sensible person."

To Michael's surprise, she agreed with him. "You're right, of course. I didn't mean to sound disparaging. I think your profession is most honorable."

One more quick glance showed him that she was smiling behind the veil and it was all he could do to keep from breaking into a face-splitting grin at her praise.

There was something impish yet charming about the banker's daughter. Always had been, if he were totally honest with himself.

Someday, Michael vowed silently, he would find a suitable woman with a spirit like Tess's and give her a proper courting. He had no chance with Tess herself, of course. That went without saying. Still, she couldn't be the only appealing lass in San Francisco. When he was good and ready he'd begin to look around. There was plenty of time. Most men waited to wed until they could properly look after a wife and family.

If he'd been a rich man's son instead of the offspring of a lowly sailor, however, perhaps he'd have shown a personal interest in Miss Clark or one of her socialite friends already.

Would he really have? he asked himself. He doubted it. There was a part of Michael that was repelled by the affectations of the wealthy, by the way they lorded it over the likes of him and his widowed mother. He knew Tess couldn't help that she'd been born into a life of luxury, yet he still found her background off-putting.

Which is just as well, he reminded himself. It was bad enough that they were likely to be seen out and about on this particular evening. If the maid Annie Dugan hadn't been along for the ride, he knew he'd have had a lot more questions to answer; answers that could, if misinterpreted, lead to his ruination. His career with the fire department depended upon a sterling reputation as well as a Spartan lifestyle and strong work ethic.

Michael had labored too long and hard to let anything

spoil his pending promotion to captain. He set his jaw and grasped the reins more tightly. Not even the prettiest, smartest, most persuasive girl in San Francisco was going to get away with doing that.

He sighed, realizing that Miss Tess Clark fit that flowery description to a *T*.

Tess settled back on the velvet tufted upholstery in the rear seat of the cabriolet and watched as they finally turned south on Van Ness and approached the center of the city. The streets in this district were well lit and broad enough to accommodate plenty of traffic, yet still seemed terribly crowded.

Parallel sets of trolley tracks with a power line buried between them ran down the center of the thoroughfare. These lines sliced their way through the cobblestones in much the same way the cable for the cable cars did, except for the fact that the trolleys were driven by electric power. Traffic increased rapidly and included quite a few of the infernal motorcars that Michael had spoken so strongly against.

Tess leaned forward and placed one gloved hand on the low back of the seat near his elbow while pointing with her other. "There's an automobile. And two more. See? They seem to be much easier to maneuver, particularly over the ruts of the streetcar tracks, no matter how the driver approaches them."

"That's only because most buggy wheels are narrower," he argued, carefully maneuvering the cabriolet between a parked dray and one of the modern streetcars as it passed. "I can't believe how some people drive with no concern for anyone else. It's little wonder there are so many accidents these days."

"Father says the motorcars will put an end to that because there won't be any horses to get frightened and bolt." She noted how hard Michael was working to control her spirited mare in the presence of the unusual, sputtering vehicles. Some of the other teamsters were having similar difficulties. "See what I mean?"

"All I see is that there's probably not going to be a good place to leave this rig near the pavilion," he replied. "Would it be all right if I let you ladies off near the door and then looked for a spot around the corner? There should be more room on Market Street, as long as the drovers have their cattle rounded up and moved on by now."

"Of course," Tess said, hoping her inflection wouldn't inadvertently reveal a desire to remain near the handsome fireman. "You can stop anywhere. I see the banner. This is where we belong."

"In your opinion." Michael huffed. "I don't believe I have ever seen so many women gathered in one place before. There must be thousands."

Tess tensed. "Wait. How will you find us again if we go inside without you?"

"I don't know. If you weren't wearing that enormous hat I could probably spot you in the crowd by your pr— By your hair."

"You were going to say pretty, weren't you?" She smiled, amused by the way his cheeks grew more ruddy in the light from the streetlamps surrounding the enormous meeting hall.

"It would be wrong of me to mention such things, Miss Clark."

That made her laugh softly. "But I would find it delightful if you did. Does that embarrass you, Michael?"

"Of course not."

He brought the buggy to a halt as close to the curb as possible, then quickly helped both young women alight and saw them to the curb before once again climbing into the driver's seat.

"Take off your hat after you get inside," he called over the din of the crowd. "I'll find you."

She knew that her eyes must be twinkling because she was keenly amused when she shouted back, "And how will you do *that,* sir?"

Michael paused just long enough to lean down from his perch and say more privately, "By your beautiful, dark red hair." Then he flicked the reins and the horse took off.

Beside her, Tess heard Annie sigh. "Oh, my. That man's smile could melt butter in the middle of winter." The shorter girl had clasped her hands over her heart and was clearly mooning.

For some reason Annie's overt interest in Michael needled Tess. She knew it was foolish to allow herself to be bothered, since the maid was a far more likely social choice for him to make than she was.

Nevertheless, Tess was surprised and a little saddened

by a twinge of jealousy. What was wrong with her? Was she daft? Just because a man was stalwart and handsome and so glib-tongued that his very words sent shivers up her spine, it didn't mean that she should take his supposed interest seriously. After all, she was a Clark, a member of the San Francisco upper crust. And as such she did have a family reputation to uphold whether she thought it a silly pretense or not.

Standing tall and leading the way, Tess gathered a handful of skirt for ease of walking and crossed the lawn to the wide entry doors of the meeting hall. There were ladies from all walks of life proceeding with her in a flowing tide of gracious yet clearly animated womanhood, she noted, pleased and energized by the atmosphere.

Perhaps this suffragette movement would remove some of the social stigmas that had always set her apart from many of her good sister Christians like Annie, she mused. If it did nothing else, she would be forever grateful.

Michael worked his way slowly south on Van Ness Avenue and turned onto Market Street. As he had hoped, there was plenty of room there for the Clark buggy. He tipped a small boy in tattered knee britches and a slouchy cap to watch the rig for him while he was gone, then headed back for Mechanics' Pavilion at a trot.

He hadn't gone a hundred yards when a man grabbed his arm and stopped him. It was one of his fellow firemen.

"Hey, Michael, me boy. Where're you bound in such a hurry?"

Before thinking, he answered, "The pavilion."

That young man, and those with him, guffawed. "No wonder you're wearin' your uniform. If you're lookin' to use that badge to impress a good woman, you surely won't find one there. Where are you really goin'?"

"None of your business, O'Neill."

"Now, now, don't be trying to get above yourself, boyo." He laughed again, spewing the odor of strong drink on a cloud of his breath.

"Don't worry about me," Michael replied with disdain. "Just take care of yourself and don't end up in a bar fight again."

O'Neill's only reply was a hearty laugh and a slap on the back as he shared his amusement with most of the others gathered nearby.

Michael hurried away from the group of obviously inebriated men, hoping none of them decided to trail after him on a lark. It wasn't that he felt he couldn't handle himself well in any situation. He just didn't want his cronies to follow him all the way to Tess and continue their taunts, straining the difficult circumstances even further.

He needn't have worried. Getting past the crowd milling around in the street and on the sidewalks and lawn bordering the enormous Mechanics' Pavilion was so difficult, Michael doubted he'd be followed by anyone.

It was all he could do to work his way through to the meeting hall entrance. First he had to run the gauntlet of shouting, chanting, angry men carrying placards denouncing the women's movement, then convince the uniformed police officers posted at the doors that his intentions were peaceful and honorable.

"I escorted several young ladies," Michael shouted to the guards. "They're waiting for me inside. I promised to join them." He held up his right hand, palm out. "On my honor."

The burly doormen looked at each other and then back at him, clearly cognizant of his official fireman's attire. "All right," one of them said. "But any trouble from you and you're headed for the paddy wagon just like anybody else. We've got more'n one waitin' right out back."

"I promise I'm not going to be a problem," Michael vowed, still holding up his hand and doffing his hat as he sidled through the narrow space between the two broad-shouldered officers.

The door most of the women were using stood wide-open. That feminine multitude was sweeping through without being questioned, although many were casting sidelong glances at each other as if they were either worried or wary. Or both. He supposed, given that this kind of gathering was such an unusual occurrence, it was natural for some of them to be uneasy particularly if their husbands didn't know where they had gone.

On the other hand there were the stalwarts like Tess, who were obviously not intimidated by a crowd, especially not by one composed mainly of members of the fairer persuasion. How on earth could he hope to locate her among this mass of velvet and feathers, furs and veils? Surely she'd realize his dilemma and at least wave her hand in the air from time to time.

Straining with cap in hand, he stretched to his full six-foot height to peer at the seething mass of well-dressed women. Those who did not have fancy hats covered with flowers and feathers were in the minority, although there did seem to be a fair number of plainer bonnets or uncovered heads as well. That was where he'd made his mistake. By assuming that only Tess would be bareheaded, he'd become overconfident.

The press of the crowd was stifling. Various aromas of perfume assaulted him as they mixed and permeated the already overly warm inside air.

He raised his eyes to the vaulted ceiling and was in the midst of a short, silent prayer for guidance when he noticed a gallery.

As he headed for the stairway leading to the upper tier he continued to pray. "Father, I know there's no way I'll ever find Tess in this mess unless You help me." His heart skipped and hammered. "Please?"

Gaining the landing, he gripped the rail and gazed down at the rows and rows of benches facing a stage where several well-dressed but otherwise unremarkable ladies sat. If not for their position at the podium, he would have assumed they were merely a part of the audience.

Would Tess press closer to the stage so she could observe the speaker's expressions? He assumed so, given her earlier conversation and the determined way she had been behaving.

Starting at the center near the front, Michael began to systematically scan the crowd row by row. He had to force himself to take his time and study the back of each person's head carefully in spite of his burgeoning anxiety.

His "Where are you?" was spoken barely above a whisper. *There? No, that wasn't her. How about...? No.*

Jostled and pushed, he stubbornly clung to his place at the railing and prayed he wouldn't have to actually return to the ground floor and make a spectacle of himself in order to locate and be reunited with the two young women. Bringing them there in the first place was bad enough. Calling attention to such a folly would be a hundred times worse.

Michael took a sudden gulp of air. *There! Was that her?*

Maybe. Maybe not. His breathing was already ragged and his heart was pounding exactly the way it did every time he answered a fire alarm. His hands fisted on the rail. He wanted to shout out, to call to Tess. To see if it truly was her he was staring at.

Fear for her safety and well-being stopped him. There might be few folks in this particular crowd who would recognize wealthy Gerald Bell Clark's daughter on sight, but many knew her name only from the society pages of the *Chronicle*. It would be unwise to call attention to her in this unusual situation, especially since he was currently too far away to protect her if need be.

Watching and continuing to hold perfectly still, he willed the reddish-haired woman to turn her head just the slightest so he could be certain.

In moments she did better than that. Standing and swiveling while she removed her coat, she looked over the crowd behind her, eventually letting her gaze rise and come to rest on the balcony.

Michael tensed. His breath whooshed out with relief. There was no doubt. It *was* Tess.

He was about to leave his place to join her when he saw her raise her arm, grin broadly and wave to him as if she had just spotted the most important person present.

To his delight and equally strong sense of self-disgust, he was so thrilled by her candid reaction that he temporarily froze.

In all the time they had been acquainted, Tess had never looked at him that way before. *Or had she?* He blinked to clear his head and sort out his racing thoughts. No matter how hard he tried to deny it, he kept imagining that perhaps she *had* done so and he had been too blind, too dunderheaded to have noticed. Until tonight.

As he started back down the stairs to join her he corrected that supposition. It wasn't foolish to ignore Tess's apparent personal interest. In his case it was the only intelligent thing to do. Even considering her to be a mere friend could prove detrimental.

The idea that she might actually covet a deeper relationship with him was unthinkable. Ridiculous.

Nothing good—for either of them—could ever come from entertaining such an outrageous folly. Not even in his dreams.

Chapter Three

The sight of Michael gazing down upon her sent a tingle of awareness singing up Tess's spine. There was no question that it was she whom he sought. The way his countenance lit up when he spotted her removed any possible doubt. And to her chagrin, she was just as thrilled to see him.

At her elbow, Annie gave a little shriek, "Up there! Is that Michael?"

Tess cast her a stern look. "Hush. You'll embarrass him. He sees us. He's coming."

"I know." Once again the maid's hands were clasped in front of her as if preparing to pray. "My knees are knocking something awful."

"Then sit down and get control of yourself," Tess told her. "We don't want to create a scene."

Tess, too, seated herself after managing to tear her gaze from the sight of Michael Mahoney zigzagging his way through the throng to join them. It wasn't easy to keep from peering over her shoulder in anticipation of his arrival. She kept herself busy by repositioning her hat and moving the pins that had held it firmly to her upswept hairdo.

Seconds ticked by. Tess was just about to stand and look for him anew when she sensed his presence.

"Is there room for me or shall I stand at the back of the room and wait?" he asked, bending to speak quietly into her ear.

Tess failed to suppress a shiver as his breath tickled her cheek and ruffled a tiny wisp of hair. She attempted to mask her reaction by gathering her skirts and scooting closer to Annie on her right.

"We'll make room," Tess said. "Please, join us." She had expected him to immediately comply. When he hesitated, she glanced up and noticed that he seemed uneasy. "What's wrong?"

"I don't know. I just got a funny feeling."

"Probably another little earthquake," Tess said with a sigh. "I've felt several since we arrived. At first I thought it was just the press of the crowd and all the perfumery making me a bit dizzy, but once I sat down, I decided it couldn't be that."

She folded her coat on her lap and patted the small section of bench that she had just cleared. "Come. Sit down. I think they're about to start the meeting."

As Michael eased himself into the narrow space and his shoulder pressed against hers, Tess was once again light-headed. She blinked and tried to concentrate, to gauge whether or not they were experiencing more earth tremors at that very moment.

It was impossible to tell. San Francisco was so prone to such things that few citizens paid them any heed. Unless the shaking was strong enough to cause actual damage, which was rare, the local newspapers gave the quakes short shrift as well. Feeling the earth move was no more unusual than the fog off the bay or the wind that preceded a storm.

Tess would have scooted closer to Annie if there had been a smidgen of room left. Unfortunately all the benches were packed, including theirs. That was a good omen for the suffragette movement but it certainly worsened her predicament.

If only she had had the presence of mind to keep her coat on as a buffer, she mused. Not only was she starting to sense an aura of warmth emanating from Michael, she was beginning to imagine that she could actually feel the man's muscles through the gathered sleeve of her blouse. That was impossible of course, yet she could not shake the unsettling sensation.

Leaning away a fraction of an inch, she noted that he shifted his position ever so slightly, too. Although he had obviously twisted to make more room for her, he had also placed himself so he could effortlessly slip his arm around her shoulders if he so desired!

That notion stole Tess's remaining breath. In her heart of hearts she wanted him to do exactly that. In the logical part of her brain, however, she knew he would never be so bold. Getting him to escort them to the lecture was already more than she had expected. Making this into a shared, pleasurable excursion was out of the question.

The only reason Michael was even sitting with them was because he was trying to be gallant.

"You don't have to stay right here if you don't want to," Tess offered, hoping to gain a respite for her over-taxed senses and imagination without revealing her reasons for needing one. "We can meet you outside after the speaking is over."

Michael shook his head and cupped a hand around his mouth to speak as privately as possible. "I'd rather not. You are too vulnerable, Miss Clark. If anyone saw through your disguise it could pose a problem."

"I don't see how."

She noted his frown and the hoarseness of his voice as he replied, "You would be a valuable prize for anyone wanting to get back at your father or perhaps seeking a ransom."

"Me? That's preposterous."

"All the same, I'm not about to leave you. Either of you," he added, leaning farther forward to include Annie.

Just then, a portly matron in a copious cape and broad-brimmed hat paused in the aisle next to him and cleared her throat noisily.

When Michael didn't rise, she said, "I fear you have not noticed a lady in need of a seat, young man. I would think a member of a fire brigade, like yourself, would have better manners."

Although he set his jaw, he did stand, bow and reluctantly relinquish his place to the demanding woman.

If Tess had not been so relieved that he had been forced to give her some breathing space, she might have felt sorry for him.

"I'll be waiting for you right outside the south door, the one we came in," Michael had said in parting. "Keep an eye out for me."

It had eased his mind some when Tess had nodded but he was still nervous about leaving her. After all, she was naïve about the inherent dangers of gatherings such as this. At least he assumed she was.

He had occasionally seen her in the Clark family pew in church and was certain she had also attended fashionable soirees, but this kind of open meeting was totally different. Here, she might come across anyone from any walk of life. How she would handle such encounters was his main concern. If she exhibited the same high and mighty attitude he'd observed so far, she could wind up in serious trouble.

To Michael's chagrin, some of the same firemen he'd encountered earlier were gathered just outside the very door he had instructed Tess to use. That left him no option but to face them.

James O'Neill was puffing on a cigar. He began to grin wryly as soon as he spotted Michael. "Well, well. I see you were tellin' the truth. Have ye gone over to the ladies' side now?"

"Of course not. I'm just doing a favor for my mother's employer, that's all."

"Oh, and what would that be?"

Keeping his voice light and a smile in place so the other men wouldn't take offense, Michael changed the subject rather than answer directly. "Never mind that. What're all of you doing here? Did you follow me?"

"Naw. We're slumming," O'Neill replied, laughing raucously. "We decided to take a gander at the *lovely* girls." He roared with glee at his supposedly clever remark. "Have ye seen 'em? I'd sooner kiss me own sister."

"I wouldn't want to kiss your sister either—if you had one," Michael countered, joining in the laughter. "She'd look too much like you—and you are one ugly fellow."

"Well said," O'Neill shot back, clapping Michael on the back and blowing smoke rings. "C'mon. Let's go find us a good pub and get some beer."

"Can't," Michael said. "I told you. I'm working."

"Moonlighting, eh? All right. Have it your way." He motioned to his cronies with a broad wave of his arm and a slight unsteadiness in his gait. "Let's go, boys."

Michael was relieved to see them walk away without further probing into his evening's plans. He wasn't ashamed of Tess—or of Annie. He just didn't want to take the chance of having his name linked by gossip with that of the young, beautiful socialite. It not only wasn't accurate, it wasn't seemly.

Although he was successfully climbing the promotion ladder within his chosen field, that didn't mean he considered himself worthy to court a highborn woman like Tess Clark. No matter how well he rose in the fire department ranks, some facts would never change. He was who he was. That he had accomplished as much as he already had was a testimony to his zeal for the job and honest hard work.

For that Michael was thankful, because it meant he'd had no unearned favors handed to him nor had he sought any. His rank and anticipated promotion were his responsibility and his reward.

"With the help of the good Lord," he added, casting a brief glance at the cloudy night sky beyond the streetlamps and remembering his spiritual roots. His father had not imparted any belief system but his mother had made up for it with a strong faith that never seemed to waver. As far as Michael was concerned, if he could become half the Christian his mother was, he'd be in good shape.

When the elderly, spry, white-haired president of the local society for the advancement of women stood, the crowd hushed. In a clear but reedy voice she introduced Maud Younger to a roar of applause and cheering.

Tess was surprised to note that Miss Younger didn't look nearly as old as she had imagined she'd be. Her clothing was a simple but fashionable white lawn waist with vertical tucks and a dark skirt, fitted by plaiting from waist to hip that accentuated her spare figure. Her grace and regal bearing reminded Tess a bit of her own mother, although this woman was barely old enough to have belonged to the same generation.

"Good evening," Miss Younger said, her voice carrying strongly. "As many of you know, I was born and raised right here in your fair city, and although I have been traveling the globe, I feel as though I've come home when I gaze upon the bay and wharves once again." She smiled. "They smell the same, too."

That brought a wave of laughter. She waited for it to subside before continuing. "Many of you come from a background of wealth. Others don't. That makes no difference in our movement. Here, we are all sisters, all equal in the eyes of God. Our goal is to make ourselves just as equal in the eyes of our fellow *men,* which brings me to the point. We have been treated as second-class citizens for countless generations. It is time for that unfair servitude to end."

As the cheers of the crowd rose and the entire audience stood to applaud, Tess felt a surge of pride for those present. Miss Younger was right. They *were* all equal. She had felt for a long time that she and Annie certainly were. Why, they had often shared the notion that they might as well be family. This movement was the affirmation of that idea, the answer to Tess's fervent prayers for understanding and equality.

Beside her, on the aisle, she heard a muttered yet clearly derogatory comment. Wide-eyed, she turned to the portly woman who had usurped Michael's place, studying her features closely for the first time. "I beg your pardon?"

"It's that evil harridan up there who should beg all our pardons," the matron said, frowning and pointing to the stage. "Does your father know you're here?"

"What?" Tess squinted at the round, jowly face. "Do I know you?"

"You certainly should. My husband and I see you every Sunday in church."

Recognition buzzed at the fringes of Tess's mind the way flies worried a horse's flanks in the summer. There was a fair chance that she had encountered this particular person in the past but she couldn't attach a name to that memory. "I'm so sorry, Mrs.…"

"Blassingame. Mrs. Henry Blassingame. But never you mind," the woman said, gathering herself as if she were a mother hen with ruffled feathers. "You just watch your p's and q's, young lady. Mark my words, this whole movement will do nothing but cause trouble."

Tess faced her nemesis as the applause died down, determined to give as good as she got. "You don't see yourself as equal to me, Mrs. Blassingame? That's a pity."

"Well, I never…" The woman spun and shuffled up the aisle, her skirts swinging from side to side like a huge, clanging bell.

Tess felt a tug on her skirt from Annie and resumed her place on the bench.

"We should go before she tells your father," the maid said with unshed tears glistening. "The Blassingames are rich enough to have a telephone. If she rings him, he'll discover we're gone."

"I'm not afraid of Papa," Tess said, although she did feel an undeniable twinge of nervousness. She smiled for

Annie's benefit. "If you're worried, then we'll go home now. I'm sure that will please Michael, too."

"There's another meeting tomorrow night and the night after," Annie offered. "Maybe you can get someone else to take you."

Starting down the aisle, Tess lightly grasped her friend's arm with one hand and carried her heavy coat draped over the other. "Don't you want to come with me, too?"

"Mercy, no."

"Why not?"

"Because it seems so wrong," Annie said, speaking quietly aside. "Look at all these women. They should be at home with their families. I know some must have husbands or children. That's where their duty lies."

"Can't they be individuals as well?" Tess asked. "I believe I am."

"Of course you are. You have all the money you'll ever need. But I don't. I never will. Neither will my poor mother, and if folks get all riled up about this suffragette movement, there's no telling how it will affect the likes of us."

"You're really afraid?"

Annie nodded vigorously. "Terrified is more like it."

"Then I apologize," Tess said tenderly. "I should never have insisted we come. I'm just so used to the two of us doing things together, I never thought about how being here might feel to you. I certainly didn't mean to make you uncomfortable. How can I make it up to you?"

"Pray. Hard," Annie said. "That's what I've been doing ever since we left your estate."

"Good idea. Oh, dear. Look."

Pausing at the archway of the exit door, Tess peered out at the milling crowd that awaited them. She and Annie were the only ones leaving early and without the buffering presence of the other women inside the hall, they were going to have to run a gauntlet of angry husbands, fathers and brothers. Even those men who were merely standing there smoking and chatting with their cronies had begun staring as if she and her frightened maid were escaping criminals.

Tess had Annie help her don her bulky black coat before she turned and squared her shoulders. Facing such a show of strength and greater size, she felt minuscule but she was not about to let any shred of apprehension show.

Head high, she walked directly into the fray as if she expected the group to part the way the Red Sea had for Moses and grant her unhindered passage. To her surprise and delight, the closest men did just that.

Chapter Four

Michael saw Tess coming. Before he could reach her and Annie, however, they had been accosted by several of the angry men who'd been lurking amidst the crowd.

He had to push his way through to get to the women. Tess was standing her ground but poor Annie was cowering and weeping into her hands.

"Shame on you," Tess shouted at their nearest adversaries as she pulled the crying girl closer. "See what you've done? You're nothing but a bunch of nasty bullies."

Hearing that kind of talk made Michael cringe. He clenched his fists as he joined the young women and quickly placed himself between them and their antagonists. Surprise was on his side. Numbers were not. He was only one man and there were at least five of the others, two of whom looked able to defend themselves most adequately.

He slipped his arm around Tess's shoulders, including

Annie in the embrace as best he could and said, "Sorry boys. My sisters need to be getting home. C'mon, girls. Papa's waiting."

It didn't surprise him one bit when Tess tried to twist out of his grip as he began to shepherd them away.

"Let go of us," she grumbled, loud enough to be heard by almost anyone within twenty or thirty feet.

Michael grinned over his shoulder at the other men and shrugged as if silently appealing for sympathy. The ruse worked. They started to chuckle and one of them gave him a thumbs-up.

Beside him Tess continued to make loud, intemperate statements as he hustled her along the sidewalk. "Stop this. I demand you release me, Michael Mahoney. Do you hear me? There is no need for strong-arm tactics. I can take care of myself."

"Oh, yeah?" He lowered his voice. "And how were you going to get away from that confrontation back there? *Talk* them out of it?"

"I was handling the situation quite adequately."

"That wasn't how it looked to me," he argued.

Deciding that they were out of danger, at least for the moment, he slackened his hold and Tess immediately shook him off.

She paused long enough to straighten her hat, withdraw one of the long pins that had held it in place and brandish the thin shaft like a sword. "See? I could have defended myself."

"For about two seconds, until one of those fellows

disarmed you." He eyed the flimsy weapon. "Put that away before you hurt somebody."

"You mean like you?"

"Yeah, like me," Michael answered. "You seem to be having trouble telling your friends from your enemies these days and I'd just as soon be out of reach if you suddenly decide I'm one of the villains."

"According to Mrs. Blassingame, that woman who took your seat, it's Maud Younger who's evil. Imagine that."

"I can. Easily," he countered. "Almost any man out here would agree." He knew he'd spoken too candidly when he saw Tess's eyes narrow. Although she did stick the hat pin back where it belonged, her motions were abrupt and jerky, indicating that her temper was far from soothed.

She grabbed Annie's hand and forged ahead with the girl in tow. Rather than object, Michael fell into step in their wake. Their party was now far enough from the pavilion that they wouldn't automatically be connected with the ongoing suffrage lecture if they happened to be observed. That was a huge relief.

"Turn right at the corner of Market," he called. "The buggy is down about half a block. You can't miss it."

Although Tess didn't answer, he noted that she was heeding his instructions. *Fine*. Let her brood or fuss and fume or whatever else she wanted to do. As long as she went straight to the cabriolet without getting into any more trouble on the way, he'd be satisfied. It had been sheer folly to let himself be talked into making this trip in the first place. The sooner it was over, the happier he'd be.

Tess would have given a month's allowance to have had another handy mode of transportation. Oh, she knew she could hire a hack to deliver her and Annie to the top of Nob Hill or even take a streetcar part of the way. It wasn't that. The problem was, she had to see to it that her father's rig was returned promptly and in apple-pie order. He was rightly proud of the sleek black, covered buggy with its deep green trim and bloodred upholstery, as well as his fine stable.

The bay mare that they were driving tonight, however, was technically Tess's. It had been a birthday gift, although her father still acted as if he were lord and master over his entire domain, including all the horses, even hers.

Without waiting for assistance she approached the side of the cabriolet, hiked her skirts, placed a booted foot on the small step and reached for a handhold with which to pull herself aboard.

The oversize coat was a bother because it hampered her freedom of movement. Nevertheless, she did not intend to stand there and wait for a bossy man who obviously didn't think she could take care of herself.

She grasped the slim metal roof supports with gloved hands and pulled herself up. Or tried to. She did lift partway off the ground but that was as far as she got. Not only was she stopped abruptly when a portion of the hem of her coat was caught beneath her boot, that yanking action caused her to lose her grip.

Tess was badly off balance before she even realized she'd made an error. Arms cartwheeling like the blades of a misaligned windmill, her body stretched and began a slow motion, backward arc.

Annie screeched. "Look out!"

Tess gritted her teeth. In the split second it took her to realize what was happening, she barely had time to hope her fall wasn't going to harm her best friend.

Gasping once, Tess stifled a scream. She threw her arms back to try to catch herself, fully expecting to feel the impact of the cobblestones through her skirt and petticoats as she landed.

Then, suddenly, she was caught up in strong arms that swung her away from Annie and safeguarded them both.

"I've gotcha. You're okay," Michael said, sounding breathless.

Tess's instincts for self-preservation kicked in and she sensibly looped one arm around his neck to stabilize herself. That brought their faces closer together than they had ever been before.

Her eyes widened. The brim of her elaborately decorated hat was the only thing keeping them apart and she could feel his warm breath through the veil.

She wanted to speak in her own defense, perhaps even to chastise him for taking such liberties. But no suitable words came to her, nor could she seem to find enough fresh air to satisfy her needs.

Michael stared into her eyes. He was not smiling. "Are you all right, Miss Clark?"

Tess tried to take another usable breath, this time succeeding. "Yes." It was hardly more than a hoarse whisper.

She found it impossible to look away, to tear her gaze from Michael's. Eyes that she had always known were a rich brown had become bottomless pools of indescribable emotion. Their eddies whirled, drawing her further and further in until she was as lost in their depths as a hapless mariner abroad in a hurricane.

Still, Michael held her close. Neither of them moved. Neither spoke. Tess noticed for the first time that she was actually embracing him and she knew it was wrong to continue to do so. She was also unwilling to relax her hold even a smidgen.

It was Annie whose words finally brought Tess to her senses. The girl grasped her sleeve. "Miss Tess! Are you all right? Are you faint?"

"No." The denial didn't sound nearly as firm as she'd intended. She began lean sideways and to push her rescuer away. "I'll thank you to put me down."

"Gladly." Michael set her on her feet so abruptly that Tess swayed for a moment. Although she knew instinctively that he was close enough to catch her again if she faltered, she was determined to thwart any such efforts.

Instead, she reached for Annie's hand to steady herself. "My coat was caught. I think I may have stepped on the hem. I'm fine, now."

"I know. I saw," Annie said. "I'm so sorry. If I'd real-ized sooner I'd have helped…"

Behind them Michael cleared his throat. "If you ladies are through making apologies, I suggest we be on our way. Once that lecture is over and the crowd disperses, we could be delayed a long time by traffic."

"I agree," Tess said.

She took the hand he offered, careful to keep from looking directly at him as she gracefully gained her seat and scooted over to make room for Annie.

What on earth had just happened between her and Michael? She could barely think, let alone recall every-thing that had transpired. He had caught her and kept her from falling, of that she was certain, but in the ensuing seconds something extraordinary had passed between them. Something she had never before felt with anyone, let alone an appealing man like him.

There had been a depth to their poignant bond that was inexpressible. And he had felt it, too. She knew he had. Chances were good that he'd be able to con-tinue to mask his emotional involvement but she wasn't fooled. She'd seen it in his eyes, had felt it in the way he'd held her close. Michael Mahoney had been every bit as touched as she had and no amount of rational thought was ever going to convince her otherwise.

Rational thought? Tess had to smile. There was noth-ing rational about the way she was beginning to feel about Michael. On the contrary, if she had been anyone but who she was, she might have been foolish enough to imagine she was falling in love with the handsome fireman.

That was impossible, of course. Tess's smile waned. She sighed. Some things might be changing in the way women perceived themselves but certain constraints of society could never be breached. One of them was the proper choice of a mate. She had standards to uphold. Duties to fulfill. She had already taken on some of the tasks inherent in running her father's home, such as acting as hostess when he entertained the hoi polloi of San Francisco. There was no way to continue to do that if she turned her back on her place in the normal scheme of things.

A sadness settled over Tess the way the fog often shrouded the bay. Why was it so easy for her to accept Annie and others like her, yet fail to fully accept the person she herself really was?

Michael didn't speak to his passengers again until he brought the buggy to a halt in front of the Clark estate. The way he viewed the situation, the less he tried to explain, the better. Besides, he hadn't had time to sort out his thoughts regarding the astounding way Tess had reacted when he'd raced to the rescue and caught her.

I couldn't stand back and let her fall, he insisted, wondering if perhaps he should have done just that. He was beginning to see that his strong sense of chivalry might prove to be his undoing—unless he was very, very careful in the future.

It was going to be at least another year, maybe longer,

before he'd be financially able to support his mother. If she lost her job at the Clarks' before that time, it would be a serious hardship. And if Gerald Clark had the slightest notion that his only daughter was being squired all over San Francisco by his cook's son, that was *exactly* what would happen.

Michael steeled himself for the berating he was certain Tess would deliver in parting. As long as he remained duly deferential, no matter how much it hurt his pride to do so, he figured the evening would end fairly well, considering.

As he prepared to help the ladies disembark, a young groom joined him and took hold of the mare's bridle.

Michael first helped Annie down, then offered his hand to Tess. So far, so good, he thought. Then he made the mistake of looking into those lovely eyes once again. They glistened like fresh drops of rain on a rose. And her cheeks reminded him of the velvety pink petals.

He blinked to clear his thoughts, to refocus on the task at hand without making a worse fool of himself than he already had. Unfortunately for him, Tess smiled and his heart sped as a direct result.

"Thank you," she said pleasantly as she stepped down. "It was good of you to agree to accompany us this evening."

Michael bowed slightly and released her hand, backing away as he did so. "My pleasure, ladies."

He heard Annie make a sound that reminded him of wind whistling through a nearly closed window sash. Tess, on the other hand, laughed demurely.

He arched a brow. "Did I say something humorous?"

"Yes. But you did it in a very gentlemanly manner." She giggled behind her hand. "I'm sorry. It was just so plain that you didn't want to go, it tickled me to hear you claim it was your pleasure."

"Perhaps it was the good company I enjoyed rather than your destination." The instant Michael heard his words he rued them.

"Perhaps."

"Or perhaps I simply like driving a nice rig." He gestured at the mare. "That's a fine animal."

"Yes. She's mine."

"Really? If you chose her, you did well."

"Thank you." Instead of leaving him and going inside, she walked to the horse and began stroking its sleek neck with her gloved hand. "Actually, she was one of my father's but I asked for her for myself. He finally gave her to me on my sixteenth birthday."

"Nice gift," Michael said, thinking about how little he was able to afford to give his mother no matter how much he wanted to please and honor her. In contrast, the gift of such a magnificent horse only served to point up the difference between his and Tess's lives.

"I can have one of the stable boys drive you home, if you'd like," Tess offered.

Michael shook his head. "That won't be necessary. I'm used to walking."

"And it's almost all downhill from here."

Boy, is that the truth, he thought, biting his tongue

to keep from speaking his mind. It would be downhill for him for sure if he did what his heart and mind kept suggesting. The mere idea of pulling Tess Clark into his arms and kissing her rosy cheek the way he wanted to was enough to make him blush as well as tie his gut in a knot.

It was also a clear warning. There were few things he could do that would be worse than acting the swain. As a matter of fact, right then he couldn't think of anything that would be more foolish. Or more appealing.

He touched the brim of his cap politely and backed farther away. "I'll be saying good night, then."

"Good night," Tess replied.

Michael knew he had to be imagining the tenderness in her tone and the personal interest in her charming gaze. If there was something unusual there it had to be that she was toying with him, pretending to care to lead him on so she could have a good laugh at his expense.

Well, that was never going to happen. He might be a tad smitten if he were totally honest with himself, but that feeling would pass. Tess would never know her flirting had affected him at all, let alone given him thoughts of courting. He was too smart to yield to such impossible yearnings. Too smart and too determined to triumph on his own. He didn't need anyone's influence or money to succeed. He was well on his way to becoming a captain. Nothing else was as important as that.

Not even love?

His jaw clenched. The clomp of his boots echoed hollowly on the sidewalk as he began to trot down the hill toward home, back to the reality that was his daily life. There was no way that he might care that much for Tess, nor she for him. Love was an overrated emotion, anyway. His mother had always insisted that his father had loved her, yet Michael had never seen him demonstrate anything but disrespect—when he was sober. When he was drunk, which was most of the time, he was just plain cruel.

That was another reason why Michael wanted to succeed. It was his fondest wish to provide well for his mother in her old age. She had worked tirelessly to raise him, practically alone, and she had earned a rest. Soon he'd be able to give it to her. Soon he'd get the promotion he'd been working so hard for.

He slowed his pace and began to whistle a tune. His life hadn't been easy but he'd come a long way since his upbringing as one of the immigrant children who were disparagingly called wharf rats. Someday, Lord willing, he'd be able to put that all behind him and never look back.

Chapter Five

Tess was barely inside the cavernous foyer of the family mansion and was standing in front of the mirrored hall tree removing her hat when she heard a familiar, attention-getting cough.

Annie immediately hiked her skirts and fled up the side stairs toward her own quarters.

Tess whirled to face the source of the cough. "Good evening, Father. How are you?"

"I might ask you the same thing," Gerald Clark said. He hooked one thumb in his vest pocket, took a puff of the fat cigar in his other hand and blew out a smoke ring as he eyed his daughter from head to toe.

"I'm fine, thank you," Tess replied. She would gladly have retreated to her room if her father had not placed himself directly in her path. To her chagrin, he was taking note of her meager disguise.

"Have you no decent wrap? I thought you had a much more suitable coat than that old one."

"It was mother's," Tess said.

"I'm well aware of that." His eyes narrowed in a scowl while he took in the familiar hat with its special, jet pin as part of the decoration. "Are you mocking me?"

Tess's heart melted and she put aside her personal concerns in order to comfort him. "Oh, Father, it's nothing like that. Honestly." She stepped close enough to briefly pat his free hand. "We—Annie and I—just wanted something dark and unremarkable to wear into the city. I never intended for you to see us dressed like this. I would never do anything to hurt you. Surely, you know that."

"I had thought so, until now," Gerald answered. "Would you care to tell me why you chose to go out so late in the evening?"

There was nothing Tess could honorably do but answer truthfully. She busied herself removing her gloves so she wouldn't have to keep staring into his face, wouldn't see his disappointment when she confessed.

"It was all my idea. I wanted to hear Maud Younger speak at Mechanics' Pavilion and Annie was good enough to accompany me." She looked up in time to see a flush of color start rising in the older man's face.

"So I have been given to understand."

"Then you know I'm telling you the truth."

"Yes. I find your actions quite disappointing. What do you have to say for yourself?"

"Nothing. I didn't do anything wrong or unseemly. The crowd was very large and I'm sure my presence went unnoticed, at least for the most part."

"You will not go again," her father said flatly.

That was his normal manner of making his wishes known, yet this time it rankled Tess more than usual. "I cannot promise that," she replied, feeling a surge of power accompanied by an equal amount of foreboding.

"What?"

If Tess had thought his face flushed before, it was pale compared to the way it looked now. She could almost imagine jets of steam escaping from his ears. "I don't mean to be disrespectful, Father, but there is nothing bad about my attending meetings composed of genteel women, and I shall do so again if I choose."

"Bah." He bit down on the end of the cigar and kept it clamped between his teeth as he glared at her.

There had been many instances in the past when Tess had cowered under her father's powerfully intent stare. Not this time. Although she hadn't stayed for Miss Younger's entire lecture she had been impressed by the atmosphere of freedom within the hall. That and the suffragette pamphlets she had read and reread so many times that they were almost falling apart had given her inner strength.

Tess straightened her spine, nodded and took a few steps, sidling past her father to start up the spiral staircase. "I respect and admire you, Papa," she paused to say. "Please try to afford me the same."

She didn't look back and heard no comment in her wake. By the time she reached the sanctuary of her private suite and closed the outer door behind her, she was trembling at the thought of what she had just said and done. Still, she had succeeded. She had politely stood up to her father and he had not screamed or cursed at her the way he sometimes did the servants. As far as she was concerned, that had been a big, big step toward her eventual emancipation.

Sighing, Tess leaned her back against the door. *Praise God.* Not only had she managed to temper her father's expected wrath, she had done so without having to mention Michael Mahoney's participation in the evening's escapade. For that, she was most thankful of all.

Given the way her heart leaped at the mere thought of that attractive man, she was afraid her father—and anyone else who saw her—might discern that she was enamored with Michael to the point of idiocy. She could still imagine the sensation of being held in his strong arms, of feeling his breath on her cheek, of yearning to be near him every moment.

Heart pounding, breathing shallow and ragged, Tess fought to subdue her roiling emotions. What was wrong with her? Was she becoming unhinged? Scripture plainly warned against coveting and that was exactly what she was doing.

Is it wrong to merely daydream? she asked herself. Surely not. After all, if people had no lofty dreams and aspirations they would never accomplish anything of value.

"Yes, except this is an impossible dream," she whispered into her otherwise unoccupied boudoir.

She knew her conclusion was right. She also knew that

she dared not confess her foolish imaginings to anyone. There were some things, some very personal things, that must remain private. Tess had shared many secrets with Annie Dugan, especially during the recent years after Mama's passing, but this ridiculous infatuation would not be one of them.

It occurred to Tess to wish that Michael would take serious notice of Annie instead, but she found she couldn't carry through with an actual prayer for such a thing. Seeing him courting the maid—or anyone else for that matter—would be like the thrust of a dagger through Tess's tender heart.

Breathless, she stood quietly and tried to understand why she was so overcome with unfathomable emotion. She had been acquainted with Michael for at least six years, ever since her father had hired Mary as their cook, yet she had never viewed him this way before.

She and Michael had talked and joked and had even engaged in innocent child's play as youngsters, such as the time they had been verbally sparring in the kitchen and she had blown a handful of flour onto his dark, wavy hair, then had laughed and run away.

Michael had chased and caught her in the rose garden, holding tight to her wrist so she couldn't have escaped no matter how hard she'd struggled.

"Let me go!" Tess had screeched, trying her best to twist free.

"Not on your life." He had been laughing, too, as he had shaken his hair and spread a dusting of the flour onto her blue frock. They had laughed, chased, played. Had a perfectly wonderful time until Mary had called out to them, stopped the tussle and scolded her fun-loving son.

Now, however, even the memory of those sweet, innocent times was enough to make Tess tremble anew and yearn to see him again even if he paid her no attention whatsoever. Truth to tell, she mused, the less special attention he paid to her, the better for all involved.

That was an unarguable fact. So why was she having such a hard time convincing herself to accept it as the most sensible choice?

When Tess awoke the following morning she was still reliving every wonderful event from the previous evening, especially the trip to and from the pavilion.

Pulling back the heavy drapes at her window, she stood for a moment to bask in the welcome rays of sun that had finally burned through the dreary fog. It was easy to compare that kind of contrast to the way she'd felt before and after she'd nearly taken a tumble and had spent those blissful few moments resting in Michael's arms. It was as if her whole life had been suddenly filled with a brightness so intense it was almost painful.

Dressing alone because she'd sent Annie back down the hill to visit her widowed mother, Tess descended the wide, sweeping staircase. First she'd breakfast with Father in the formal dining room the way she normally did. It might be trying to carry on a pleasant conversation after his negative reaction to her actions last night, but facing him this morning would help her discern whether or not he was still upset.

Entering the large, formal dining room she paused, puzzled. There was a floral centerpiece with unlit tapers standing tall and stately at each end of it. The handmade damask and lace cloth beneath was pristine, as always. However, the room was not occupied. Papa was not seated at the head of the table. Nor was there the usual silver coffee service waiting for him on the buffet.

Her breath whooshed out all at once when she realized what that meant. Papa had eaten early and left!

Immensely relieved to postpone facing the one person she never seemed able to fully please, Tess swept past the table with a lighter heart and lithe step and pushed the swinging door to enter the kitchen.

The cook looked up with a smile.

"Good morning, Mary."

"Morning, miss. You heard that Mister Gerald has already had his breakfast?"

"I saw he was gone, yes." Tess knew she was grinning foolishly but she couldn't help herself. She'd fretted for hours the night before, anticipating a confrontation with her banker father, and it looked as if he'd put aside his displeasure—at least enough to go about his normal business rather than dally to chastise her. Annie would be very glad to hear that, too.

"I believe I'll take my breakfast right here with you," Tess told the cook.

The woman's astonished expression made Tess giggle and ask, "What's wrong? Does it bother you?"

"No, miss. I'm just surprised, is all. You haven't been visiting me much since you got too big to beg sweets."

"I'll never be too old for that." Tess pulled up the same stool Michael had used the day before, sat down and leaned her elbows on the table in spite of knowing it was poor etiquette to do so. "I like it here. I can relax and not worry about how I sit or how I eat or anything else. Can you understand that?"

Mary smiled and her apple cheeks brought happy crinkles to the corners of her brown eyes. "Aye. I've often wondered how ladies like you can stand to be laced up so tight and sit so proper all the time. I'd think it would be a terrible trial."

"It is." Tess accepted the cup of hot coffee Mary placed before her with a pleasant "Thank you."

"You're welcome, miss."

Although Tess had always felt at ease in the kitchen, whether she was grabbing a cookie or maybe sampling the upcoming meals, she could tell she had just taken another step forward in her relationship with Mary Mahoney, especially judging by how the older woman was smiling down on her.

"Your dear departed mother used to visit me this way," Mary said. "Especially when…"

"When she knew she was about to pass?" Tess asked, her smile growing wistful.

"Aye. Mister Gerald didn't want to listen to how she really felt so she'd come out here sometimes and talk to me. She was a lovely person." The cook blinked back unshed tears. "And now that you're grown, you're the spitting image of her."

"That's what everyone says." Moved, Tess paused to sip her coffee and used the time to compose herself. "I do miss her. It's only been a little over four years, but there are times when I try to picture her face or recall the sound of her voice and I can't quite do it."

"That's all right," Mary said. "Remembering the love is all that counts. She loved you dearly."

"I don't know what I'd have done if I hadn't had my Annie to listen to me back then. It's no wonder we've grown so close."

"Where is Annie?" Mary looked past Tess toward the main part of the mansion. "Isn't she hungry, too?"

"If she is, her own mother will be fixing her something," Tess said. "She got so homesick after we'd been into the city last night, I sent her off to Mrs. Dugan's early this morning. We had hoped to see her mother at the lecture but the crowd was so huge there was little chance of finding anyone in that mass of humanity."

"Scrambled eggs all right?" Mary asked with her back to Tess.

"Yes, thank you. And in case you were wondering, Michael did a fine job as our chaperone."

"I didn't want to ask."

Tess chuckled. "I could tell. Actually, he ended up scolding me worse than Papa did when I got home."

"Oh, dear."

The cook's concern made Tess laugh more. "Don't worry. I didn't take offense." *And he also caught me when I almost fell. It was wonderful,* Tess added to herself, lowering her lashes to stare into her coffee cup rather than let her gaze meet Mary's and perhaps reveal too much.

"Good. I'm sure my son was only thinking of what was best for you."

"So he said." Tess felt her cheeks warming so much that she was certain it showed.

"Are you going back again tonight?" Mary asked.

That notion had already occurred to Tess. Her problem was not being able to count on Annie as a companion and proper chaperone. "I don't think so."

"'Tis a pity."

"Why?" Surely, Michael had not expressed any desire to repeat the previous evening, so Tess was at a loss to understand the underlying reason for Mary's question.

"Because I'd like to see what all the fuss is about," the cook said with a slight smile. "I wouldn't want to go alone, of course, but I thought…"

"I'd *love* to go with you," Tess said, beaming. "What a wonderful idea."

"Mister Gerald wouldn't mind?"

"I've already warned him that I might attend again. I know he'll approve of my choosing a sensible, mature woman like you for a companion."

"Then it's settled." The cook slid Tess's eggs onto a plate, added a warm biscuit and delivered the meal to the table.

When she paused there, Tess looked up at her with a smile. "Is there a problem?"

"Only with me old coat and hat," Mary said. "'Tis good enough for church but I don't want to embarrass you."

"Anything that's good enough for the Lord is certainly good enough for me," Tess said. "If it really bothers you, though, I do have another coat and hat you may wear and then keep, if you like. They belonged to my mother."

"Oh, I couldn't."

"Nonsense. Annie wore them last night and they were too big for her so they should fit you perfectly. They're still up in my room. I know Mother would want you to have them in any case."

"It's a darlin' girl you are," Mary said. "Your mama would be very proud."

"I truly hope so," she answered wistfully. "I wish she were still here so I could ask for her advice."

"Could ye ask me?"

Tess almost choked. More warmth flowed into her already rosy complexion and she shook her head as she clasped her hands and bowed over her plate to ask the blessing.

Some of the most troubling elements in Tess's life were her errant, possibly sinful thoughts of Michael Mahoney. Confessing as much to the man's mother was *not* on her list of suitable ways to cope. Not even at the very bottom of that imaginary list.

When the telephone at Michael's fire station rang, the last person he was expecting to hear from was his mother. "What's wrong, Ma? Are you sick?"

"No."

"Then why are you calling? I didn't think you were allowed to use the Clarks' telephone."

"Miss Tess gave me permission and showed me what to do."

"Great. So, what's wrong?" He was imagining all sorts of terrible catastrophes, all beginning and ending with Tess Clark.

"Nothing. I just wanted you to know not to stop by tonight, in case you don't have to work, I mean. I won't be home after supper."

"Why not?"

"Because Miss Tess and I are going back to the Mechanics' Pavilion and…"

Michael couldn't contain his astonishment. "What? Are you daft, too?"

"Don't be silly. And don't be talkin' that way about Miss Tess."

"I suppose she's standing right there listening."

"Yes. And she's a fine lady."

"She's more like a spoiled brat," Michael argued, only half agreeing with himself.

"I'll pretend I didn't hear you say that, Michael Mahoney, and I certainly hope she didn't, either. Now put that Irish temper of yours back in your pocket and calm down."

Grumbling under his breath, Michael managed to control his gut-level response. If that impulsive young woman dragged his mother into trouble he'd never forgive her. Never.

"How are you getting to and from the pavilion?" he asked.

"I don't know. We'll be fine. Don't worry yourself one little bit."

He wanted to warn her to be careful, even toyed with the idea of ordering her to stay home. But he knew his mother. And he was beginning to know Tess a lot better than he'd planned to. Neither of them was the kind of woman who could easily be bossed around, although of the two, he figured his mother would be the more tractable.

"All right. Do as you please. Just stay together and don't talk to strangers. Hear?"

As she ended the conversation and hung up, Michael almost thought he heard giggling on the other end of the line. That was not a good sign. Not a good sign at all. It probably meant that his mother and Tess were sharing a laugh at his expense.

"O'Neill," he called up the narrow wooden stairs that led to the firemen's quarters on the second floor. "I'm going to need you to take part of my shift for me tonight."

There was a moan, followed by, "Aww, me head's splittin', Michael."

"It's your own fault if it is. Sleep it off till supper time. I'll wake you before I leave."

"What's so all-fired important? You got another moonlightin' job like last night?"

Michael huffed and answered under his breath, "No. This one's even worse."

Chapter Six

Since her father had objected to her wearing her late mother's favorite coat the evening before, Tess had replaced it in the attic chest. As she'd carefully folded the garment and prepared to lay it back in the trunk, she'd noticed a thin, linen-covered book tied with a satin ribbon. She hadn't seen that for years. It was Mama's journal.

Touched by nostalgia, Tess had intended to leave the precious book where it was, unread, but at the last moment she'd snatched it up, carried it to her room and slipped it under one of the feather pillows on her bed.

Now, dressed in her own elegant broadcloth coat with a velvet shawl collar and a much more demure chapeau bearing a few white feathers and small pink roses, she was ready for her evening adventure.

Michael had had so much trouble finding a place to leave the buggy the night before, Tess had decided it would be smarter to not use the cabriolet again that evening. She hoped her companion wouldn't object.

"I don't mind a bit," Mary said, buttoning the fitted, hand-me-down woolen coat as she and Tess prepared to leave the house. "I walk into the city all the time."

"I wish I could say I did," Tess replied. "Father has always been too protective for that. I've never had the opportunity to explore much farther than the church over on Van Ness, at least not by myself." She smiled as she paused on the back porch and donned kid gloves. "I suppose you think that's odd."

"Not for the likes of you, it isn't. Mister Gerald is just looking out for you. He always has."

"It feels more like being a prisoner," Tess said with a sigh. "I know he means well, but…"

"Aye. They all do. It's the way they were raised, more's the pity. Take my Michael, for instance."

Tess's heart leaped in spite of her desire to keep from reacting to any mention of the man. "What about him?"

"He wasn't truly angry when I told him where you and I were going even if he did sound that way. He was just being bossy, like his father was, God rest his soul."

"I've never asked you about him. I'm sorry. Has your husband been gone long?"

"Long enough," Mary said with a soft sigh. "He wasn't gentle like my son but I know he did the best he could for us."

Hearing Michael referred to as *gentle* seemed odd to Tess. She thought of him as strong, stalwart and very masculine. Then again, she supposed a man's mother would view him in a different light than others did.

"I could hear the rise of Michael's voice when you told him where we were going tonight. He certainly didn't sound very happy."

That made Mary laugh. "I think they're all petrified that we women will stop takin' their orders. We won't, of course."

"Oh, I don't know," Tess said. "That notion does sound appealing."

She looped her arm through Mary's as they descended the sloping drive onto Clay Street and turned toward Van Ness. It seemed a bit strange to be on foot, let alone in the company of the estate cook, yet Tess's heart was light and her enthusiasm boundless.

The sun had set. A row of gaslights lined the upper portion of the avenue between the trees, illuminating their pathway. Fog was thin and patchy this evening which also lent an air of openness. Homes they passed were, for the most part, well-lit as well, thanks in part to the proliferation of Mr. Edison's electric lamps, especially in the wealthier parts of the city where the gas along the streets had also been replaced by electric lamps.

As an added plus, a warm breeze was blowing over the inland hills so the air was merely tinged with salty sweetness instead of bearing the unpleasant aroma that often rose from the docks, especially during the summer.

Tess sighed happily. This was true freedom. A simple change of habit had shown her a whole new world; a world where she could just be herself rather than Gerald Bell Clark's pampered daughter. It was an amazingly liberating feeling, one she found so exhilarating it nearly stole her breath away.

Michael had changed from his fireman's uniform into the black corduroy suit he wore when attending church, hoping to blend in better. If he'd had an Ulster overcoat such as his father had worn, he'd gladly have donned it, too, to ward off the evening's chill.

He joined the throngs of men once again milling in front of the pavilion. His dour mood fit the overall atmosphere perfectly. Hatless, with his thick, dark hair slicked straight back, he thrust his hands into the pockets of his suit coat as he paced, waiting and ruing the confrontation he knew was coming.

As before, the crowd was swelling with women from all walks of life, including society matrons, although he assumed that most of them were simply out for a lark rather than convinced that this crazy idea of equality for women had real merit.

Scanning the multitude, he spotted his mother before he saw Tess. Mary was taller in the first place, and since she was wearing an ornately flowered and beribboned hat that added nearly another foot to her height, she certainly did stand out above the crowd.

Elbowing his way toward her, Michael noted that Tess was at her side. He forced a smile and greeted them amiably. Or so he thought.

"Good evening, ladies."

Mary gasped.

Tess frowned before replying, "What are *you* doing here?"

"Looking out for the pair of you, if you must know," he said.

"We don't need looking after." Tess's chin lifted and she stared at him. "We are perfectly fine on our own."

"That's a matter of opinion."

"Yes, it is," Tess said. "Mary tells me she often walks about in the city. Alone. If you're not concerned about that, you certainly shouldn't worry about us when we're together."

Michael's jaw gaped. She was right. His mother did make a practice of strolling the city streets, at least some of them, unescorted.

"Not after dark, she doesn't," he countered.

Tess glanced at the well-lit pavilion and then gave him a self-satisfied smile. "It's hardly dark here, sir. Now, if you will excuse us, we'll be going inside."

Without thinking, Michael reached for her arm as she tried to pass.

Someone else tapped him on the shoulder from behind at the same instant.

As he turned to see who was interfering, he saw a flash of movement and felt a jolt to the side of his jaw.

Staggered, Michael released Tess. He blinked to clear his swimming head. A mustachioed dandy in a bowler hat and striped silk cravat was facing him with fists raised defensively, posing like a boxer in the ring. The man was jumping around on the balls of his feet as if there were swarms of biting ants inside his shoes.

"What the…" Michael began.

Tess raised her voice and interrupted with a sharp "No!" She stepped in front of him. "Are you all right?"

"Yes." Nevertheless, he rubbed his jaw and peered past her while Tess turned to face the attacker, her hands on her hips.

"Phineas Edgerton. What in the world do you think you're doing?"

"Defending your honor, Miss Clark." He stopped dancing around but didn't lower his fists. Nor did he take his eyes off Michael. "G.B. told me you might be here tonight."

"My *father* sent you?"

"In a manner of speaking."

"Well, go home. There's no need for you here. And certainly no call to go around punching innocent people."

In Michael's opinion, the man Tess had called Phineas was not planning to take her seriously. He was of a slighter build than most firemen and clearly not much of an adversary in a real fight. Still, he had delivered a hard enough blow to temporarily stun and Michael was not about to give him a chance to do it again.

When Phineas reached toward Tess, Michael acted. He pushed the thinner man away with more force than was needed and sent him reeling.

"Stop it. Both of you." Tess raised her arms and intervened as if attempting to keep two brawling little ruffians apart. "This is ridiculous."

Although Michael did give ground he remained ready to renew the battle if need be. "We'll see about that."

"No. You will see nothing." Calmly and deliberately, she nodded at the other man. "Phineas, may I present Michael Mahoney and his mother, Mary."

To Michael's dismay, he had temporarily forgotten that his mother was even present, let alone standing back and watching the whole confrontation.

"Mary, dear, this is Mr. Edgerton, one of Father's vice presidents," Tess continued.

The cook made a slight curtsy but did not offer her hand. Neither did Michael.

Tess went on, "I suggest we all go inside and find suitable seats before they're all gone." That said, she slipped her hand through the crook of the banker's elbow and motioned to Mary to do the same regarding Michael.

He offered his arm to his mother without hesitation. As long as Tess and that skinny fop were going into the lecture hall, he might as well accompany them.

Later, when he had a chance to speak to his mother in private, he intended to tell her exactly what he thought of her foolishness. Going to a controversial lecture like this was bad enough without joining forces with the boss's daughter to do so. There would be no way that Gerald Clark would not hear every juicy detail, thanks to his toady.

Michael clenched his fists. He wished he'd punched Phineas in the nose instead of merely giving him a shove.

He sawed his jaw from side to side to test it. Unless he

missed his guess, he was going to be sporting a dandy bruise on his chin by tomorrow. That was what he got for letting himself be dragged into another of Tess's wild schemes.

Beside him, his mother tightened her grip. When he glanced down at her she peeked from beneath the brim of the fancy hat. "Your Irish is showin'," she said, giving him a sly grin. "You'd best mind your manners if you want to impress anyone."

"Only you, Ma," Michael said. "You know you're my best girl. Always will be."

Mary chuckled. "I surely do hope not. I have me eye on a houseful of grandbabies just as feisty and handsome as you are."

Tess was walking several paces ahead of mother and son and the crowd was creating a loud murmur that kept her from overhearing everything they said. The few words she had picked out, however, were enough to make her blush. Unlike Mary, Papa had never mentioned the next generation, nor had he pushed her to court more often than she had wished to. At least not yet.

Eyes downcast, she glanced at the expensively tailored coat sleeve where her gloved hand rested and recalled a few times when this man's name had come up in conversation. It was starting to look as if it was no accident that her father had chosen to send Phineas on this particular errand. He was young, single, well-born and a rising star in the banking business. Not only that, the Edgerton family was one of the richest clans on the west coast.

Tess shivered. Surely Papa wasn't trying to play matchmaker. Or was he? It would be just like him to try to manipulate her into joining two prominent families through matrimony, for the sake of increasing the influence and holdings of both.

Pulling her hand from the banker's sleeve, Tess eased away from him.

"Is something wrong, Miss Clark?" he asked, doffing his bowler and removing his gloves now that they were inside the hall.

"No. Nothing. It's just very crowded in here, don't you think?" She dropped back until she was beside Mary. "I see the front rows are already full. Shall we sit back here?"

"Fine with me."

To Tess's chagrin, the older woman immediately edged into the nearest row and led the way.

Both men stepped back politely, eyeing each other like two feisty roosters in a barnyard. Tess balked. According to proper etiquette, she should follow Mary. That would place her between Michael and his mother, or, even worse, would leave poor Phineas sitting next to her on one side with the surly fireman on his other.

She glanced back and forth, unable to decide what was the best move. Michael looked ready to explode and Phineas was acting so proper and stuffy she wanted to shake him.

Her eyes locked with Michael's and she tried to will him to understand. It almost seemed as if he did comprehend her dilemma when he bowed slightly and said,

"If you all will excuse me, I'll be waiting for you ladies outside like I did the last time."

Tess wanted to thank him, to let him know that she was grateful for his sensible choice. Unfortunately, she had no chance to speak before he quickly wheeled and stalked back up the aisle.

Phineas, however, seemed smugly satisfied, giving her further proof that he was far too much like her father to suit her. He gestured for her to follow Mary, then, hat and gloves in hand, joined her.

Having that man seated so close felt nothing like it had to have Michael beside her. There was no thrill, no warmth, no sense of strength or power. Phineas was simply there.

If she hadn't been with Mary, Tess would have left the lecture hall and abandoned the unpleasant man without a moment's hesitation. Her wish to do so doubled when Phineas leaned closer and whispered, "What did that ruffian mean by *the last time?*"

Tess merely folded her hands in her lap, faced forward and pretended she hadn't heard the question.

To Michael, standing idle outside, it seemed as if the meeting was lasting forever. He hoped his mother had gotten the women's movement out of her system by now. He'd certainly had enough of it.

The whole premise was crazy. Women had men to take care of them. They didn't need to be standing on a soapbox and yelling for more rights. It was bad enough that there were already a few female dentists and doctors practicing in the city. Why, a committee of misguided ladies had even petitioned the Board of Supervisors to allow women in the police department a few years back. Next thing he knew, they'd be wanting to join the fire brigades!

A stir near the wide sets of double doors drew his attention. They swung open and hoards of excitedly babbling women began to exit the hall.

Michael stepped up on the base of the monument to labor so he could peer over the heads of other men.

He spotted his mother, Tess and that despicable little banker in moments.

Shouldering his way through the crowd, Michael quickly joined them. If Tess was surprised to see him she gave to indication of it.

"I'll walk you home," he said.

"That won't be necessary but we do thank you." Tess smiled slightly. "Don't we, Mary?"

"Aye. We know the way. You can go back to work, son."

"I got O'Neill to cover for me," Michael explained. "I don't have to report back till morning."

Tess's smile spread. "Well, it won't take us *that* long to walk the few blocks home, even if it is mostly uphill."

Next to her, Phineas cleared his throat. "Ahem. I have a carriage waiting, Miss Clark." He fidgeted and ran a finger beneath his starched collar as if it was choking him. "I, um, well, I didn't know you'd be with anyone. It only seats two."

"Then I know there will surely be plenty of room for

you to ride alone," Tess said, reaching to pat the cook's hand. "I shall walk with my friends."

It didn't escape Michael's notice that she had said *friends,* not *friend.* Good. The young woman might be capricious but she was definitely loyal. If she had gone off with that weasel of a banker and left his mother to trudge home alone, Michael would not have thought well of her. Not well at all.

To his delight, Phineas appeared to be struck dumb.

"Shove off, man," Michael told him. "You heard Miss Clark. She has no further need of you."

"Well, I never…"

"No, you probably haven't ever been talked to this plainly before. 'Tis high time you were."

In the background, Michael was certain he heard Tess's familiar giggle when the other man turned and stomped off. That laugh warmed his heart. Obviously she wasn't angry with him. What a relief.

Now, his biggest remaining concern was his mother's welfare. When her boss got wind of her nighttime outing with Tess, there was sure to be a blowup. He just hoped and prayed it wasn't going to cost her a job she loved and the rooms she occupied in the servants' wing of the estate.

When he offered his arm to Mary, Michael was astounded to feel Tess fall into step on his opposite side. She was not only grasping his elbow as if they were promenading, she was grinning beneath her thin veil.

He chanced a smile in her direction. "I take it you

weren't disappointed that your beau had no room for the likes of us."

"Oh, dear. I hadn't thought of it that way but you're probably right. Phineas is terribly snobbish." She huffed. "And he is certainly *not* my beau."

"I take it he believes he has your father's blessing to court you."

"Then Father is sadly mistaken," Tess replied. "I have no beau, nor do I seek one. The more I hear about women's rights, the more empowered I feel."

"You have no desire for home and hearth?" Michael asked, feeling his mother squeezing his arm as he spoke.

"I didn't say that, exactly." Tess gathered her skirts in her free hand to keep them out of her way as they began to ascend the steeply sloping avenue. "I simply see no pressing need to swoon at some gentleman's feet and pretend I am in need of sanctuary."

"I see." It was all Michael could do to keep from chuckling at her naïveté. She had grown up so cosseted by her father she saw herself as far more independent than she truly was. If Gerald Clark had not been exercising his control over her, he would not have bothered to send an emissary to the suffrage lecture to do his bidding and to squire Tess home.

Expanding upon that thought was sobering. G.B. had his fingers in plenty of political pies in city and county government, including the upper echelons of the fire and police departments. If he took a notion to sabotage a promotion within one of those organizations he would probably succeed.

When Mary asked that they rest for a few moments so she could catch her breath, Michael decided to use the opportunity to voice his concerns to Tess in the hope she would understand.

"I want to ask a favor," he said.

"Really?" Lifting the veil, she placed it atop the hat and looked directly at him. "All right. Ask away."

"I'd like you to make certain that your father doesn't blame me or my mother for your transgressions."

"And just what would those be?"

"This evening. And the one before," Michael said, gesturing at the pavilion that lay behind them at the foot of the hill. "He's a powerful man. If he thought we had led you astray he might not be very forgiving."

"Nonsense," Tess said flatly. "Annie said the same thing. You're all wrong. Father isn't vindictive. He may be stern but he's fair."

Although Michael nodded and dropped the subject he didn't stop wondering if Tess was fooling herself. G. B. Clark's reputation painted him as anything but evenhanded.

If he failed to be fair-minded, or if he refused to believe his daughter's claim that these nightly jaunts had been her idea, there was no telling how far the ripples of discontent would extend. Or who they would harm.

Chapter Seven

Tess would have loved to attend every lecture Maud Younger gave in the City by the Bay. What she didn't want to do was push her father too far, too fast. A week after her last trip to the pavilion she was still waiting for him to mention Phineas and chastise her for her behavior.

So far Papa hadn't said another word about the incident, not even when their pastor's Sunday sermon had dealt with forgiveness. Waiting for her father to finally get around to mentioning her transgressions was harder for Tess than being immediately scolded would have been.

As a result she had been unduly nervous when she entered the dining room each ensuing morning for breakfast.

Today, her father was dressed in a neatly tailored gray, pin-striped suit and vest that almost matched the color of his moustache. He sat at the far end of the massive, linen-covered table, his visage hidden behind a fresh copy of the *Chronicle*.

Tess skirted the table to pour herself a cup of hot coffee from the silver service on the buffet rather than wait to be served. As she took her place at the opposite end of the long table she peeked around the floral arrangement and said, "Good morning, Father."

Gerald Clark merely grunted. That kind of reaction was far worse, in her estimation, than his angry words would have been. He had never been one to chat unless the subject of a conversation was finance or something else of equal interest to him, but his recent actions, particularly toward her, had seemed more off-putting than usual.

Looking for a way to draw him out and bring things to a head, Tess asked, "So, how is Phineas Edgerton doing these days? You haven't mentioned him much lately."

With that, the newspaper was partially lowered. Gerald peered over the top edge, his bushy gray brows knit. "If you must know, he is nursing a broken heart."

"Why?" Tess felt herself beginning to frown, too, and carefully schooled her features to eliminate any sign of negativity. "Surely he can't still be upset that I declined his offer to drive me home."

"He can and he is," her father replied. "That was cruel of you, Tess."

Astounded, she stared. "Cruel? Phineas intimated that I was welcome to ride with him but my companions were not. *That* was the cruel thing."

"What? You expected him to give way to servants?

It's bad enough that you persist in treating Annie Dugan as an equal. The girl is your maid, Tess, not your friend, and it's time someone reminded you of your place as well as hers."

"Annie is a truer friend than any of the other young women I know."

"You see? That's what I've been trying to say. Your mind has been poisoned by that drivel you've been hearing at those idiotic lectures."

"I respectfully disagree."

Rising, her father crumpled the paper and his napkin next to his plate and faced her, his moustache twitching as his jaw clenched repeatedly. "There is nothing respectful about the way you speak to me, girl. I suggest you remember who supports you, who buys you those expensive gowns and pretty trinkets you love so much."

Tess fingered the dainty pearl earbobs that were her favorites. Other than those, the only jewelry she wore regularly was the cameo pinned at the high, ruffled neck of her blouse. That brooch had been her mother's.

"I do appreciate your generosity, Father," she said, struggling to sound normal in spite of wanting to shout, or weep, or both. "It was Mother who loved jewelry and furs. I ask for very little beyond my daily needs."

"Bah!" Muttering under his breath, Gerald Clark stalked from the room, leaving Tess to wonder if she should wait there for his possible return or if she dared head for the kitchen where she knew she'd find sanctuary with Mary.

She fidgeted, counted slowly to one hundred, then made up her mind. In a few quick steps she'd made good her escape.

"There may be extra duty to be had tonight," Michael told O'Neill. "We'll both need to be alert."

"Why? You plannin' to start some trouble I don't know about, boyo?"

"No. It's because of the crowds expected at the Grand Opera House. Caruso's singing."

"I'd lots rather hear a good *Irish* tenor," O'Neill said, grinning. "Those Italians are too full o' themselves to suit me."

That comment made Michael laugh. There were many immigrant populations in San Francisco and each thought it was the most important. He supposed that was normal, yet he wished they could all work together better for the common good. If the various factions weren't at odds with outsiders, they were busy squabbling amongst themselves. As far as he was concerned, it was wasted effort.

Stepping out onto Howard Street in front of Station #4, he looked at the Chinese laundry across the street, then turned and raised his gaze to encompass the expensive homes on Nob Hill to the north. It would be at least three more days before his usual visit to his mother and he'd had to miss last Sunday's services because of a small fire at Meigg's Wharf, so he hadn't seen Tess in over a week. Not even from a distance.

Would she be one of the opera patrons at the special

performance tonight? he wondered. Perhaps. And if so, whose arm would she be on? If it happened to be that young banker's, as he suspected it might, Michael was not going to be pleased.

He snorted in self-derision. Who was he kidding? The only person he wanted to visualize standing beside Tess Clark was himself. He could easily imagine her lovely blue eyes twinkling at him; her lips curving gently in a smile that warmed him through and through no matter how cold the wind off the Pacific happened to be.

That dream was never going to come true, he concluded, so why waste time envisioning it?

Deep in thought, he circled the narrow, three-story fire station building and entered the ground-floor stables from the rear.

The behavior of the usually placid fire horses drew him back to reality. They seemed unduly agitated. Since there had been no recent alarm, there was no reason for them to be behaving as if they were about to be harnessed to one of the steam pumpers and race off to a fire.

Approaching the nearest gray gelding, Michael stroked its neck to calm it as he pictured Tess ministering to her mare the night he had driven her into the city. Her touch had been gentle but firm. She had the ways of a true horse lover and he admired that about her.

"As well as plenty of other things," Michael muttered, continuing to soothe the nervous animals as best he could. Several of them were prancing around in their stalls as if they were about to try to kick their way out. That was odd.

He raked his fingers through his thick, dark hair as he pondered the animals' unrest. They sometimes behaved this way after a slight earthquake and he assumed he had simply not been as aware of the shaking as the horses were. If so, they'd soon settle down. They always did.

Going about his chores, he fed and watered the teams, then sauntered back into the front portion of the station where the captain's scarred oak desk, a telephone and the red-enameled alarm box sat. Duty rosters were pinned to the walls next to a calendar from one of the banks G. B. Clark didn't happen to own. A pair of narrow windows flanked the front door. Because this room was so close to the stable and a live boiler also sat in the basement, it smelled more like a steamy barn than an office.

It wasn't much to covet. Nevertheless, it was Michael's goal to lay claim to it soon. Aspiring to the next rank made a suitable goal for the present. And maybe someday he'd be the kind of chief engineer who inspired his men to loyalty and valor the way Dennis Sullivan did.

The Sullivan family had their own private quarters over on Bush Street, Michael reminded himself. Quarters suitable for his mother and perhaps a family of his own, as well.

His only problem seemed to be an inability to picture any woman other than Tess Clark in the role of his wife.

"I wish I could take you with me to hear Caruso tonight," Tess told Annie. "But since I can't, I want you to go visit your mother again. You might as well stay over till morning."

"You'll need me to help you undress when you get home," Annie argued, shaking her head. "That gown is mighty tight."

"I can manage. If I get stuck I'll call Mary. Once I loosen this horrid corset I'll be fine." She tried to take a deep breath and failed. "If I don't swoon first."

"You look beautiful in that shade of green," Annie said. "The velvet shimmers when you move."

"I know. I love it." Tess patted her highly upswept hair and pivoted in front of the mirror so she could see the emerald and exotic-feather-decorated clip her maid had added at one side. "I just wish…"

Annie giggled. "I know. You wish you could show Michael Mahoney."

"I wish nothing of the kind!"

"Oh, then why are you blushing?"

Tess made a silly face and turned away. "I'm not. This outfit is simply constricting my breathing and I am a bit faint."

"Balderdash. You always blush terribly when anyone mentions that man. Admit it. You're fond of him."

"All right. I may care for him a bit. That doesn't mean I intend to get serious."

"Have it your way. You talk a good fight but you retreat the minute the tide turns against you."

"This tide has always run against me," Tess said sadly. "I am who I am. Nothing can ever change that."

"Maud Younger disagrees."

"Yes, but she has determined to remain single and dedicate herself to the cause of freedom and equality for all. I agree with her in principle. I just don't feel that strong a personal calling."

"Meaning?"

"Meaning, it would please me to someday marry and have a family," Tess said, staring out the window of her room without really seeing the city below.

Annie gasped, muting the reaction by pressing her fingertips to her lips. "You aren't considering that horrid Phineas person, are you?"

"No. Of course not. But until my father finds someone else, I've decided to make the best of it. Phineas will be meeting Father and me at the opera tonight." She made a face. "I've perfumed a lace hanky so I can breathe its lavender sweetness if I'm too overcome by his presence."

"I don't think a bucket of cologne would be enough to help me tolerate that man," Annie said. "You are much stronger than I am."

Tess shook her head gently, taking care to keep from dislodging her elegantly coiffed hair. "Not really. I pray all the time that the good Lord will spare me from having to marry such an odious man. There must be someone waiting for me, someone who will please God, my father *and* me."

"That's a tall order," the maid said, "but I will pray for it, too."

"Good." Tess reached for her white fur cape and the small, beaded bag containing her opera glasses. "And while you are praying, please ask that I will remain in control of my temper tonight. If Phineas tries to take liberties, I fear I might want to give him the same as he gave poor Michael the last time they met."

Annie gasped. "You wouldn't!"

"No, of course not." She smiled wryly. "But that doesn't mean I would not be sorely tempted."

It wasn't within Michael's jurisdiction to stand across from the opera house and watch the carriages and motor-cars of the elite arrive to discharge their wealthy passengers. Instead, he had to be satisfied to position himself at the corner of Howard and Seventh streets so he could see all the way up to Mission.

He knew that unless the Clarks' driver was forced to circle the block there was little chance of catching even a glimpse of Tess. Nevertheless, he felt compelled to try.

Tess would be beautiful, of course. That was a given. And even if he failed to actually see her he could always imagine her loveliness the way he did nearly every waking moment, not to mention in his fondest dreams.

Michael no longer had any doubt he was smitten. Although he and Tess had been acquainted for years and had played like siblings when they were younger, he had only recently realized what an admirable woman she had become. It was undoubtedly just as well that he had moved into the fire station to live four years ago, before Tess had matured enough to catch his eye. If he had still lived under the Clark roof there was no telling how hard he would have had to struggle to keep his distance, especially if she had shown the least interest in him.

Was she interested now? He couldn't help but wonder. After she had asked him to be her escort to the lecture it seemed as if something important had changed between them. Was he imagining that she now looked at him fondly? Was he fooling himself that there was tenderness in those expressive, blue eyes when they met his? Surely not.

Michael shrugged. What difference did it make? He was a working man and she was an heiress. There was no chance, none at all, that he could ever hope to climb the ladder of success enough to be considered her peer, let alone earn enough to support her in the manner to which she was accustomed. And he would never accept money from her. Not under any circumstances. He had his pride.

Watching the slowly moving parade of elegant carriages and a smattering of automobiles turn onto Mission Street, he scanned them carefully, looking for the fancy cabriolet he had driven when he had been with Tess and Annie. When he finally spotted it, pulled by a brace of matched bays this time, he thought his heart might pound out of his chest.

The Clarks' driver was easing the sleekly polished rig between two smaller buggies when a motorcar passed in a sputtering, smoky roar, frightening several teams besides his and causing them to fight the harness traces.

Michael ran forward, leaped the tracks to dodge a

clanging electric streetcar, and raced to Tess's rescue without a thought for his own safety.

He grabbed the horses' bridles and held on to the team for dear life, fighting against their desire to break free and run amok with the Clark carriage and its passengers.

Like the horses in the fire station, these animals seemed unduly fractious. "Easy, easy boys," Michael crooned. "Settle down now. Settle down."

Although the danger from the near accident was over in seconds, several nearby drivers continued to have trouble controlling their teams as well.

While Michael stood holding the horses, he saw Gerald Clark, in black tie, tails and shiny top hat, climbing down and offering his hand to the most beautiful vision of womanhood he had ever laid eyes on.

"We'd better walk from here or we'll be late for the opening curtain," the older man said, paying little attention to the uniformed fireman who had so gallantly come to their assistance.

Placing her hand in Gerald's, the woman gracefully disembarked. The flaring hem of her fitted emerald gown flowed around her ankles like sea foam on a beach after a storm. She wore elbow-length white gloves and a white fur cape that made her cheeks look like orchids nestled in the snow.

And her hair! Michael could hardly tear his gaze from that magnificent reddish hair. It glowed with inner fire and its curls and waves shimmered like polished brass. The jewels that adorned it accented her beautiful eyes, yet the glistening gems paled in comparison to Tess's natural beauty.

Instead of letting her father escort her all the way to the curb, she paused and faced Michael.

"Thank you for tending to the horses, sir," she said with a smile and a tilt of her head. "We could have been upset—or worse—if you hadn't stepped forward."

He nodded, touching the bill of his cap with his free hand. "My pleasure, ma'am. A lot of these horses seem hard to handle tonight."

"I had noticed." She lagged as her father began to urge her past. "Why do you think that is?"

"I don't know." Michael was so entranced he could barely think, let alone make polite conversation. This was the very chance he'd hoped and prayed for and there he stood, practically speechless.

"You're the prettiest girl in San Francisco tonight," he finally said aside, hoping that the street noise would keep his comment from being easily overheard, especially by her father.

Tess laughed gaily and glanced back over her shoulder at him as she walked off. There was a twinkle in her eyes. "Only tonight?"

Before Michael had a chance to answer, she was too far away to have heard him unless he had shouted. That would have been foolish. And highly improper. After all, what woman in Tess's position would want a passerby shouting to her about her beauty?

He waited until the Clarks' driver was ready, then released the team to him and returned to his former place on the sidewalk across the street. There was no need to stay away from the fire station premises any longer, although there was no current need for his services. He had seen what—who—he had been waiting for.

And he knew in his heart that he would never forget the way Tess had looked tonight. He'd meant every word he'd said. She was the most beautiful woman he'd ever laid eyes on, in San Francisco or anywhere else.

And when she had smiled at him with those dancing eyes and that impish expression that said far more than mere words ever could, he'd felt as if he were the only man in the world.

As far as he was concerned, Tess Clark might not be the only woman but she was the only one who mattered.

Chapter Eight

Gerald Clark, imposing as ever in his starched white ruffled shirt with diamond studs, pleated velvet cummerbund and tailcoat, greeted Phineas Edgerton in the lobby, as planned, making Tess's stomach lurch.

She accompanied her father up the stairway to his private box while trying her best to ignore the other man. They all waited while an attendant drew back the heavy, tasseled curtain that served as its door.

Following her father into the box, she was amazed by the garlands of real orchids, roses and narcissus that festooned the curved balcony of not only their box but all the others, as well as decorating the leading edges of the stage and orchestra pit. The embellishment made the opera house look like a beautiful garden and the scattered petals of fruit blossoms perfumed the air most deliciously.

Unbidden, Phineas cupped her elbow and guided her to a chair next to the larger one that was always reserved for her father. Once she was settled, the younger banker collapsed his top hat and placed his silver-handled cane across the closest seat at her other hand, clearly appropriating it for himself.

"Are you comfortable, my dear?" Phineas asked, hovering as he helped her off with her cape and draped it carefully over the back of an empty chair.

Tess merely nodded, feeling so trapped she was ready to scream and seeing no way to escape, gracefully or otherwise. As far as she was concerned, being sandwiched between her father and Phineas Edgerton was akin to being laced into her corset. The sooner she could be free of all of them, the happier she'd be and the better she'd be able to breathe.

Withdrawing her ebony and silver, engraved opera glasses from the beaded bag, she raised them and concentrated on watching the stage as the orchestra finished tuning up and the overture began.

"I was delighted when G.B. asked me to accompany you this evening," Phineas leaned closer to say.

All Tess did was lift a gloved finger to her lips in a plea for silence. To her relief, he settled back in his seat and stopped trying to engage her in conversation.

Watching the performance, Tess imagined herself as the gypsy, Carmen, with Michael as Don Jose. Except that she would never lead the man she loved astray like that, nor would she turn from him to another man the way she knew Carmen eventually would.

At intermission, Tess politely excused herself and left Phineas and her father behind in the box, insisting with a demure blush that she had no need of an escort to the powder room.

Her thin satin slippers made no sound on the thick carpet as she hurried quickly, gracefully, to the multipaned window at the end of the hallway. That alcove was located close to the ladies' room door so she figured she could always duck in there if anyone happened to question why she was prowling the halls alone.

She'd gone to that window specifically to look down on San Francisco. To seek another glimpse of her personal Don Jose. The city below was well-lit and bustling with activity, as expected. Would Michael still be lingering on the corner where she had last seen him? Probably not. Nevertheless, she had to look.

Shading her eyes from the dancing flashes of light from the crystal prisms on the electric lamps behind her, she studied the street. It was no use. If Michael was still among the pedestrians she was unable to pick him out from so far away.

Tess folded her gloved hands and closed her eyes to pray, "Father, please tell me what to do. How can I let Michael know that I care?"

Unshed tears gathered behind her lashes as she pictured the gallant fireman. "And keep him safe, Lord. Please? He's in danger all the time and I would die if anything happened to him."

That heartfelt, honest prayer became her answer. She loved Michael. Period. If only she could run to him right now, throw herself into his arms and tell him… *Tell him what?*

Behind her the house lights flashed, then began to dim. It was time to return to her seat—to her father and Phineas—for the rest of the performance. For the betrayal of poor Don Jose and the eventual death of Carmen.

Tess had to force herself to take the necessary steps. She sighed as she reentered the Clark box and resumed her place. This was not the right time to act on her revelation and go in search of Michael. She had a duty to Papa to remain with him for the rest of the evening. It would cause him great worry and consternation if she left the opera house without explanation, and trying to sensibly voice what was on her heart was beyond impossible.

Not only would he have been livid as a result, she herself wasn't sure how she felt or what she might say with regard to the yearnings she was experiencing.

Enrico Caruso's continuing portrayal of Don Jose was magnificent and beautifully tragic as she'd known it would be, yet all Tess could think about was how dashing Michael had looked when he'd raced to her rescue and grabbed the bridles of the frightened horses.

As the famous tenor sang and her mind drifted with the music, she was able to couple her memories of the real hero in her life with the romantic images created onstage. Tears gathered behind her lashes once again and she tried to blink them away without letting either of her companions see that she was so moved.

Her heart soared, then plummeted, then rose again on wings of hope as the orchestra played and the magnificent voices lifted together to tingle her nerves and leave her enthralled.

Every note, every crescendo, reminded her of Michael. If this was what true love did to a person's emotions, she didn't like it one bit. How could she possibly have been foolish enough to have fallen for that man?

A lump in her throat and a shiver singing up her spine provided absolute proof. She not only could have, she had. The question was no longer what had happened, it was what she should do about it to avoid the kind of tragedy being portrayed in the final act of the Bizet opera.

By the time the curtain fell and the performers were taking their bows, Tess was no closer to a sensible conclusion than she had been before. That was the basic problem, of course. There was nothing logical about her dilemma so there could be no rational decision.

Mostly, she wanted to speak privately with Michael, although how she might accomplish that—or what she would say to him if she did—remained a puzzle. It was only Tuesday. By her reckoning it would be at least a week and a half before he revisited the estate, assuming he stuck to his usual schedule. And anything could happen to alter that.

Tess's vivid imagination pictured him meeting and falling in love with someone else in that short space of time, just the way Carmen had ultimately chosen the toreador over the soldier who had given up everything for her love.

That vivid notion pained her deeply. Not that she had

any claim on Michael Mahoney. Yet, in the back of her mind she kept hoping that something would alter their circumstances enough that they could face their attraction to each other and at least discuss it sensibly.

Women clad in furs, satin and diamonds had gathered at the base of the stage and were showering a proud Caruso with roses and effusive praise.

Yawning, Gerald Clark led the way out of the box before the applause had fully died, leaving Phineas to help Tess don her fur wrap.

San Francisco's mayor, Eugene Schmitz, a former orchestra leader himself, encountered the group in the teeming upper hallway and struck up a lively conversation with the banker.

"If you gentlemen will excuse me," Tess said with a slight smile and careful incline of her head so she wouldn't disturb her highly decorative coif, "I'll be waiting in the lobby." She fanned herself with a gloved hand for emphasis. "I must have some fresh air."

To her dismay, Phineas immediately offered his arm and stepped forward to escort her. She had no choice but to allow him to do so. Moving slowly amid the press of the crowd, they descended the staircase from the private box to the immense, vaulted lobby with its gilded fixtures, Raphaelesque murals and crystal chandeliers.

She paid little attention to anyone other than to return their polite nods or brief greetings. Traversing the plush Oriental-patterned carpeting of the staircase, Tess had to admit that briefly touching Phineas was better than possibly slipping in her new shoes and causing a scene.

The last thing she wanted was to give her father more reason to chastise her.

The lobby was teeming with opera aficionados, all praising Caruso's performance. Tess knew it was a coup to get the famous New York Metropolitan Opera Company to appear at their opera house and she was proud that her city had managed to do so for the second time.

"Wait here while I go shout for the carriage," Phineas said, patting her hand in parting after they reached the lobby level. "G.B. should be down to join you in a moment."

Tess nodded amiably. She wasn't afraid to be left alone in the midst of the milling multitude, even though a few of the attendees' outfits were not up to the elegant standards of hers and her father's. In Tess's opinion, that was a good thing. The more people who could appreciate the fine arts, the better for the city as a whole.

Spotting a sleek carriage that she assumed was hers, she clasped her cape at her neck with one gloved hand and lifted her gossamer hem slightly, proceeding out the door. When she drew closer to the street, however, she realized that she had been mistaken so she stepped out of the way to let others pass.

The foyer of the opera house was too crowded to comfortably reenter and the night's weather was fairly pleasant for a change, so she decided to remain outside to wait for Phineas and her father.

Bejeweled women swept past like the outgoing tide, most prattling excitedly about how they'd found Caruso such an enthralling hero figure. Tess smiled to herself. She'd enjoyed the opera, of course, but in her eyes there was only one true hero.

Still picturing Michael, she imagined she saw his familiar, broad-shouldered figure crossing the street and coming toward her.

Her breath caught. She pressed her hand to her throat. Disbelief was quickly replaced with delight. It *was* Michael! And he had clearly noticed her, too.

Nervous and unsure of what course to take, she edged to the fringe of the mass of exiting opera lovers and waited for him.

He rushed directly to her. The sight of him was so thrilling, so dear, she immediately offered her hand. He grasped and held it without hesitation.

"Michael," Tess whispered, knowing that there was much unsaid in her tone, in her gaze. "How did you find me in this terrible crowd?"

"I don't know," he replied softly. "I can only stay a moment. I have to get back to the station soon."

"You shouldn't have come again. I don't want you to risk losing your job."

"I won't. A friend is covering for me. I just had to see you again, to tell you how beautiful you are."

"I want to meet where we can talk more freely," Tess said quietly aside, squeezing his fingers for emphasis. "Not at the house, though. Perhaps you could send word through Mary and I could meet you some afternoon in Golden Gate Park."

"I'd like that," he said.

Before she could reply he lifted her hand to his lips and kissed the backs of her fingers through the glove, exactly the way she had seen many fine gentlemen express affection.

Tess was glad Michael was still holding her hand because she felt woozy. Her eyes widened. Then she began to smile broadly. "I wish you were the one escorting me home again this evening."

His eyebrows arched and he gave a soft laugh. "So do I, Miss Clark. So do I."

"You should call me Tess, you know."

"Should I? I wonder."

She saw his smile fade and his focus narrow as he glanced past her shoulder, then dropped her hand.

"Here comes your father. I have to go."

"Meet me? Promise?" Tess called after him as he whirled and jogged back across the street.

Although he didn't answer or even wave, she knew he would be getting in touch with her to set up their rendez-vous. What she would say to him, or he to her, when they finally did meet in private was another matter altogether. She only knew that the prayer she'd said for Michael during the intermission was already being answered. The rest of her many concerns she would also try to release and leave the results up to God.

She turned to greet her father. To her great relief he was showing no sign that he had seen who had just kissed her hand and had won her heart long before that.

For the time being, keeping her father in the dark was exactly what Tess wanted. If and when the time came to tell him of her errant heart's desire, then she would pray for the wisdom to do so prudently.

In retrospect, it was easy to imagine that God had brought her and Michael together for His divine purposes. She wasn't about to deny a providential nudge like that. She simply wasn't ready to beard the lion in his own den and confess anything to her father before she was sure it would be necessary.

Suppose Michael rejected her profession of love? she asked herself. The very thought of such a thing made her tremble but it also provided a caution against blurting out her feelings without making certain that they were returned in kind.

Michael was so engrossed in thoughts of Tess and her plea for a private meeting with him that he was back on Howard Street in front of Station #4 before he even realized he'd arrived.

What had he done? Had he inadvertently led her on?

Michael made a guttural sound of self-disgust. Of course he had. And he had no one to blame but himself. He'd given in to his desire to see Tess again and by approaching her tonight he had made her believe that his interest was too personal.

Who was he kidding? It *was* personal. And kicking himself for displaying his fondness for her so openly would do no good.

The sensible course of action was to meet Tess as she'd asked, then explain to her why they could never declare any shared affection. He could do that. He *would* do that. It was the only honorable choice.

Clenching his jaw, he entered the rear of the fire station and noticed that the horses were still snorting, shuffling and acting decidedly uneasy. When he spotted O'Neill trying to comfort them he joined him.

"What's wrong with all these animals tonight?" Michael asked.

"Beats me. I thought maybe you'd given them an extra ration of grain."

"Not me. Must be some other reason. A lot of the horses out on the streets are acting the same way."

His fellow fireman began to scowl. "That doesn't sound good. You know what usually happens when they get this upset."

"Sure." Michael shrugged off the concern. "Don't worry though. The city may shake a little from time to time but it never amounts to much. Any serious trouble we were going to have has already happened years ago." He eyed the steam pipes leading up from the boiler in the basement that they kept heated in preparation for charging the mobile pumpers with hot water. "It's not like it was in the old days before the fire brigades formed. We're ready for anything now."

O'Neill nodded. "Aye. That we are. I'll just feel better about it when these horses tell me it's safe again."

Chuckling, Michael agreed. "Me, too. In the meantime, how's your hangover? Do you want to take the watch tonight or shall I?"

"Since you let me nap away me big head all afternoon,

I think you should have the whole night to sleep, if you want," O'Neill said with a wry grin. "Callahan and I can listen for any alarms and wake you if we need you."

Michael figured he wouldn't sleep a wink because of his constant thoughts of Tess but he nevertheless accepted the offer of an entire night off. His quarters were upstairs in the station, along with those of many of the other firemen, so he wasn't far away if he was needed.

He clapped his friend on the shoulder. "All right. It's a bargain. I'm such a light sleeper I usually hear the alarm going off anyway."

"Why do you think I drink?" O'Neill asked with a grin. "Can't hardly sleep without a little medicine to calm the old nerves."

"I wish we could give some to these poor nags," Michael said with a snort of derision. "If they don't settle down pretty soon they'll be too worn-out to pull the engines."

"I know. I'll stick with 'em for a bit. Might even make me a pallet out here so I can tell if they get worse."

"You sure you don't want company?"

"Naw. I owe you. Besides, horses don't care if there's a bit of the grog on a man's breath."

"You haven't been drinking again, have you?"

"No. Not yet," O'Neill said. "But I may be sorely tempted by the time this night is over, and that's a fact."

"Well, if you do hit the bottle don't tell me about it," Michael warned, "or I'll have to report you."

"Yeah, yeah, I know. That's why you'd make a better captain than I ever would. Have ye heard anything more about your promotion?"

"No." He felt a twinge of foreboding. If he declared his fondness for Tess Clark and her father was as upset about it as Michael expected him to be, he could kiss any thoughts of rising in the fire department's ranks goodbye.

That, however, was not the basic reason why he intended to disabuse her of any notions that they belonged together. The insufficiency was his and his alone. He could never hope to attain the high station in life to which Tess belonged. And he would never presume to ask her to lower herself to his class among the more common folk. She deserved better.

"But not a man like that odious Edgerton," he muttered to himself.

Climbing the narrow wooden stairway to the common bunk area on the second story, Michael kept shaking his head in disgust. There was no way a man like him could hope to influence Gerald Clark one way or the other, so why concern himself with the possible choice of suitors for Tess?

Troubled as well as frustrated, Michael stripped off his uniform coat and boots and threw himself onto his narrow cot without bothering to finish undressing or turning down the covers. He laid his arm over his eyes to try to blot out the image of Tess being courted by anyone but him.

On either side of his bed, sleeping firemen snored

loudly. The racket wasn't enough to distract Michael's thoughts or keep him from recalling every nuance of Tess's image and every inflection of her voice when she'd begged for a meeting.

Yes, Michael concluded sadly, *I'll meet her. And I'll tell her that no matter how either of us may feel, there is absolutely no chance we can ever find mutual happiness.*

In his heart of hearts he knew that was true. But deeper, in the part of him that he suspected was his soul, he was still able to visualize putting his arms around Tess and seeing her gaze up at him with the same tenderness she'd displayed outside the opera house that very evening.

She was a vision of pure loveliness coupled with an intelligence and wit equal to any man he'd ever met, himself included. And her eyes! When she'd looked at him with such intensity, such affection, he'd had to struggle to keep from kissing her in spite of the hundreds of witnesses milling around.

Nurturing that image and letting his sleeve blot up the sparse moisture that kept gathering in his eyes, Michael finally dozed off.

Chapter Nine

April 18, 5:13 a.m.

Tess was dreaming. She was wearing her emerald-green gown again and being escorted to the opera by a tall, handsome, well-dressed man who could only be Michael Mahoney. Everyone was deliriously happy, especially her. Even Papa was smiling and holding out his hand as if accepting her choice of a beau.

Then, suddenly, the whole opera house began to quiver. When Tess tried to scream, she was mute.

Awakening abruptly, she was confused. She blinked rapidly to help clear her head and try to focus.

This was no dream. It was a true nightmare. The room was actually rocking and there was a loud, ominous rumble echoing throughout the house, as if the very walls and floors were groaning in agony.

Tess shouted, "Annie," at the top of her lungs before she remembered that she had sent the girl into the city to visit her mother, Rose, the evening before.

Fisting the sheets, Tess held on to her bedding and peered through the narrow openings between the drapes at her windows. Night was still upon them, although a waning moon illuminated the swaying trees in the formal garden and there was a glow to the east above Mount Diablo. Dawn was very near.

The ground continued to shift. It was less of a jerking motion now and more like riding the waves at sea.

Scooting to the edge of her mattress, Tess grasped the carved mahogany bedpost and hung on for dear life. The great, stone house on Nob Hill was built on firmer ground than much of San Francisco was but it still felt as if it was about to be shaken apart.

"Father!" she shouted above the roar and creaking. "Father. Are you all right?"

Gerald Clark's gruff "Yes" gave her relief in spite of its harshness. "Stay where you are," he ordered.

Tess could tell by the changing direction of his voice that he was not taking his own advice. And if he could move about, so could she.

Swinging her bare feet to the floor, she continued to cling to the bedpost, hoping to keep her balance. She reached one hand for a robe she'd left lying on a nearby fainting couch and lurched toward the door as she slipped her arms into the robe's belled sleeves.

Her left shoulder slammed into the doorjamb. Hitting that frame and leaning against it was the only thing that kept her on her feet.

After pausing to tie the sash of the pale silk dressing gown, she made her way awkwardly to the spiral staircase that lead to the main floor and grabbed the top railing with both hands. A flurry of activity was taking place below.

"Father!"

"I told you to stay in your room."

Someone had lit a few of the old gas lamps to illuminate the foyer and she could see Gerald's deep scowl in shadow as he glared up at her. His thick gray brows were knit, his grimace clearly visible.

"I'm safer down there with you," Tess argued.

"Not if this ceiling caves in."

She could see the continuing sway of the crystal chandelier above the entry hall. The heavy, ornate fixture seemed securely anchored to its carved medallion, yet there was no way to predict whether or not it was going to stay that way.

"I think the shaking is almost over," Tess said, starting to inch her way down the stairs while keeping a tight hold on the banister. "It's not nearly as bad as it was when I awoke."

"That doesn't mean the first shock is all there will be," her father insisted. "If you must be up and about, I suggest you dress properly. And tell Annie to get down to the kitchen and help Mary prepare extra meals. We may have to feed refugees."

That notion chilled Tess to the bone. Refugees? In her home? Surely the destruction of the city could not be that extensive. Plenty of previous quakes had damaged buildings here and there and had started a few fires which were quickly extinguished. That kind of repeated event, though troublesome, was easy for a city the size of San Francisco to handle, especially given the marvelously efficient fire brigades that had been organized, particularly after the mid to late 1800s.

Her breath caught. Fires and destruction meant danger for Michael! Her heart raced at the mere notion. She wheeled and started back to her room, keeping a steadying palm pressed to the hallway walls for support as she went.

Although she could dress without Annie, the usual elaborate upsweep of her hair would have to wait. Under these horrible circumstances, such trivialities hardly mattered.

"Dear Lord, watch over the firemen and all the others who are trying to help," Tess prayed, adding a silent, special word for dear Michael.

Continuing to brace herself as a different, more circular manner of shaking commenced, she staggered back to the window in her room and clung to the edges of the heavy drapes as she threw them open.

What she beheld made her tremble nearly as badly as the earthquake. Multiple small fires were already scattered across the panorama between her home and the shiny, copper dome of the new city hall. Since there was more than one blaze, she assumed the fire department's resources would be sorely taxed.

Once again the movement of the ground abated, although for how long only God knew. Grabbing the first ensemble she saw in her armoire, Tess threw on her clothing. She was buttoning the jacket to her favorite afternoon ensemble and smoothing its gray, gored skirt when she once again looked down at the city.

"Praise the Lord, some of the fires are already out," she whispered, immensely relieved. Everything was going to be all right. And as soon as Annie arrived home from her mother's, they'd both lend a hand in the kitchen, just in case Father happened to be right about refugees.

It was not beneath Tess to volunteer to do housework. She was far from the helpless female her father assumed her to be and she didn't mind proving it, especially lately. Though Mama had been frail all her life, her only daughter was a strong woman just like Maud Younger and the other suffragettes she admired so.

Someday Father would have to admit that he had raised a child who was more like himself than he'd ever imagined, Tess mused. And when that happened, she was going to be tickled pink.

The first inkling Michael had that something was very wrong was the rocking of his narrow, metal-frame cot. He'd been dreaming of being aboard a ship and had thought at first that the movement was part of that dream.

Then he opened his eyes and saw the truth painted in the dim glow of sunrise. He sat bolt upright, staring in wide-eyed disbelief.

The lanternlike lamp hanging from the center of the ceiling was swinging as if a giant hand were pushing it to and fro. He heard glass falling, windows cracking.

Tiny pieces of white-painted plaster began to rain down on him and the other firemen.

He instinctively raised his arms for protection, shouting, "Look out, boys. Take cover!"

A distant roar filled his ears, as if a hundred hissing, chugging steam locomotives were racing to converge in that very room. The sound built until it was deafening, and as it increased so did the strength, lift and drop of the tremors.

The beds began to lurch like bucking horses. Empty ones bounced higher than the others as the floor heaved, then subsided, only to do it again and again. Michael's cot inched all the way across the room before it hit an interior wall and stopped traveling.

"Dear God, help us," he shouted, noticing that many of the others were also calling out to the Almighty. And well they should. This was nothing like the other quakes he'd experienced. This one was massive. Catastrophic beyond description.

He'd just begun to think the worst was over when the movement altered and changed course, causing even worse damage. Bricks began to shake loose and fall from the outer walls into the street below.

Outside, shrill cries of injured and dying animals rose to join the cacophony of human terror. Grown men and women could be heard shrieking like terrified children.

The ground continued to tremble. The entire fire house swayed and shuddered. The nearest window popped out of its frame and disappeared in a hail of mortar, stone and brick.

Michael attempted to stand. Instead, he hit the floor on all fours. Crawling along the buckling boards, he braced his back against a wall and wriggled into his boots as best he could from a horizontal position.

Time seemed to be standing still, yet he knew several minutes must have passed since the initial shock had awakened him. This was no normal quake. This was *big*. And their problems wouldn't be over just because the trembling eventually stopped. If it ever did!

His already racing heart leaped into his throat and he breathed a name that made his gut clench. "Tess."

There wasn't a thing he could do for her—or for anyone else—until he had learned the worst and seen if he was needed on the job immediately. If he was to be held in reserve for later assignment, as he hoped he would be, the first thing he was going to do was head for the Clark estate and check on the two most important women in his life.

He suddenly remembered the telephone his mother had used to call him. As soon as he could, he'd ring the Clarks' house. He had to know for sure that she and Tess were all right.

"Father," he prayed as he staggered to his feet and lurched toward the door, hoping against hope that the stairs would still support his weight, "please look after them. Both of them."

Michael was through arguing with himself. Miss Tess

Clark was a vitally important part of his life. She always would be, whether he ever chose to admit it to her, or not.

Tess held tight to the banister, worried about another aftershock, as she made her way to the staircase and started down for the second time that morning. Father and the other male servants were no longer gathered below so she paused there to look for damage. Other than a few spidery cracks in the walls, everything looked secure.

A rising sun was peeking over the tops of the trees and beginning to brightly illuminate the east windows, making the need for artificial light unnecessary. That was good. Apparently, there was no electricity to power the chandeliers or Father would not have bothered to light the gas wall sconces.

While Tess watched, one of the closest flames fluttered as if starved for fuel. Then, the next in line began to do the same, a clear sign of danger.

Working her way cautiously from room to room, she checked to be certain that each valve was tightly closed and each switch for the electric lights was also turned off. Their house seemed to have weathered the earthquake without too much destruction but that didn't mean that the gas mains and electric lines from the city below had not suffered plenty of damage.

According to her father and his outspoken friends including Mayor Schmitz, the land under the wharves and Chinatown and even much of the downtown business district, was terribly unstable when shaken. That explained why the areas nearest the bay were always affected the most when the ground shifted.

"It must be dreadful this morning," Tess muttered to herself as she worked her way through the house, carefully skirting shattered remains of porcelain bric-a-brac and imported glassware that had once been so dear to her mother.

Keepsakes no longer held the importance they had even yesterday, Tess realized. Although the loss of such lovely trinkets saddened her, it was the other citizens whose welfare was uppermost in her mind.

Over and over she prayed, "Dear Lord, please, please help the poor people in the lowlands."

When she reached the kitchen she saw Mary peering with concern at the tall, blackened stove pipe that had been the outlet for smoke from the wood cookstove before it had been replaced by a more modern, gas model.

"Are you all right?" Tess asked, slightly surprised to note a tremulous quality to her voice.

Mary gasped, whirled and rushed to her, enfolding her in a mutual embrace of support and commiseration. "Yes. Are you?" She sniffled.

"Yes," Tess answered. "That was terrible. I thought it was never going to end."

"Aye." The older woman nodded and stepped back, looking chagrined. "I'm sorry. I shouldn't have hugged you like that. I just…"

"Nonsense. We both needed it. There's nothing like

a disaster to make everyone equal." She swiped at a stray tear sliding down her cheek. "Is everything still in working order? I saw you looking up at the flue."

"Just giving thanks that Mister Gerald installed gas for cooking, even if it was hard for me to get used to," Mary said. "That pipe shook loose. You can see the soot on the wall. I suspect we'd best not use any of the chimneys till they're checked for damage."

Tess had not thought of that kind of problem. "You're right. How clever of you."

"Just repeatin' what Michael always says," Mary explained. "He's more worried about what might cause fires than he is about earthquakes, at least he used to be. After this mornin', who knows?" She sank heavily into one of the kitchen chairs and blinked back tears of her own. "I'm fair troubled about him."

"So am I," Tess said without embarrassment. At a time like this she saw little reason to hide her true feelings. Joining Mary, she reached for the cook's hands and clasped them tightly atop the table. "I saw him last night, at the opera."

"My Michael? He was there? How? Why?"

"I was hoping you might be able to tell me," Tess said. "Has he confided in you?"

"About what?"

Here was the moment of truth, the instant when she could have made excuses and kept her opinion to herself, as before. This time she chose not to. "About how he might feel regarding me."

"No." The older woman's eyes widened. "Of course not. Why would he be tellin' me anything about you?"

"Because we have developed strong feelings for each other," Tess said. "Oh, he might deny it but I know better. I saw it in the way he looked at me last night."

Mary was shaking her head. "You were beautiful, all dressed up formal-like. Any young man would have looked on you with admiration."

"Not the way Michael did," Tess insisted. "I shall never forget the way he took my hand and kissed it."

Astonished, Mary jerked free and jumped to her feet. "He did no such thing."

It was more a question than a statement, at least that was the way Tess interpreted it. "Yes, he did. And he was so handsome and charming I wanted to forget everything else and run away with him then and there."

"Such nonsense," Mary muttered. "'Tis a terrible, terrible thing."

In spite of the recent disaster, Tess managed to smile and reply, "*Terrible* is not at all the way I would describe it. As a matter of fact, it was so wonderful I can't find words that are magnificent enough to half do it justice."

Chapter Ten

Havoc reigned in the center of the city. When Michael ventured forth he realized he wouldn't need the stairs to reach street level. He was already down there. Portions of the upper floor had fallen onto the lower one and all he had to do was step through the remains of the doorway and climb over a pile of loose bricks to reach the street!

Stunned, he stepped out and turned slowly in a circle, staring in disbelief. It was gone. The station was *gone*. The American Hotel, next door, lay in a heap, too. Its upper floors were askew and the lower ones had vanished, just as the office in the fire station had. Nearly the entire block had been flattened and the few partial walls that were still upright looked fragile enough to be toppled by a mere zephyr.

He knew at a glance that there was little difference any one man's efforts could make. Even if every able-bodied soul in San Francisco tried his best, it wouldn't be enough to alleviate this much suffering or save even half the lives he knew were presently being snuffed out like candles in a wintry gale.

His intent had been to report for duty. He would have, had there been anything left of the office at his station. The collapse of the second floor had buried the alarm system as well as the telephone he had hoped to use— not that there was even a remote chance either was still operable.

Coughing from the dust, eyes smarting, he picked his way through the rubble toward what had once been the stables, dreading what he might see and expecting the worst.

That was exactly what he found. Although all but one of the horses seemed to have broken free and escaped the carnage, the lifeless body of James O'Neill lay half buried by tons of wood and masonry. So did every single piece of their expensive fire equipment.

There was also a gaping hole over the standby boiler in the basement and Michael could see its pipes hissing and spitting streams of hot water. The only good thing about that was the moisture dribbling down and quenching the hot coals before flames could escape the firebox and cause more destruction. If more destruction was even possible.

Stunned, Michael dropped to one knee beside his friend's body and automatically checked for signs of life.

"Ah, James," he murmured. "'Tis a sad, sad day. I'm so sorry." Touching the man's exposed wrist, he felt for the pulse he knew would not be there. Tears gathered in his already smarting eyes and he heaved a sigh.

"Father, take my friend to be with You," Michael said. "He had his faults, as we all do, but he was Your child."

Rising after a quick "Amen," he did the only thing he could. He left and went to look for the rest of his comrades, continuing to ask God's favor and mercy upon them as he picked his way over and between piles of fallen bricks and stone.

To his relief, he found most of the other men gathered in the middle of Howard Street, gaping at the building that had been the pride of Company #4 only minutes ago. There, they were being formed into a loosely knit workforce by a junior officer who had assumed temporary command since their captain didn't seem to be thinking clearly.

"I just came from the stable. We've lost O'Neill," Michael announced, managing to keep his voice strong and steady for the sake of the others. "Looks like most of the horses ran off but the engines are good and buried. There's nothing left to work with. All we can do is concentrate on helping the living."

The officer gestured toward a pile of splintered wood on the corner that had been the American Hotel. "Michael's right." He pointed to individuals. "You three start digging over there where you hear cries."

Although the firemen were clearly in shock, they complied.

"What about me?" Michael asked.

"I was going to go try to find Chief Sullivan," he said, "but I'm sending you, instead. Tell him we need to know if he wants us to join another company or stay and work here, on our own."

"Do you really think it matters?" Michael asked, staring at the destruction and shaking his head as he tried to accept all he was seeing. "What if I can't find him?"

"Then do whatever you feel is right. I won't be holding my breath waiting for you to come back. At this point, we're all pretty much on our own."

"I agree."

Michael turned and started off. Stone facades of notable buildings that were now unrecognizable extended in drifts into the street. Miles of flat paving stones were buckled like crumpled paper and there was a rift in the street as if the land had been split apart by the hand of an angry giant.

The sight of water gushing from ruptured pipes within the chasm made Michael shiver. If the main supply lines had fractured, as he now believed they had, firemen would have to tap cisterns that were strategically placed throughout the city in order to get enough water to quench the fires.

Suddenly a disheveled, gray-dirt-covered young woman lurched toward him and grabbed his arm, forcing him to stop and pay attention to her. He started to explain his mission and shake her off, then caught his breath. "Annie? Is that you?"

She was muttering unintelligibly. All Michael could make out was, "Tess…"

His heart nearly stopped. He grabbed Annie by the shoulders. "Tess is here? Where?"

"She, she…"

As he watched, Annie's eyes rolled back in her head and she swooned.

He knew he couldn't abandon the helpless young woman to the milling crowds that were beginning to fill the streets. Nor did he dare place her inside one of the already tottering buildings. There were sure to be deadly aftershocks and more buildings would collapse. That was a certainty.

Just then, another, lesser quake rumbled. The land beneath Michael's feet vibrated like a bowl of warm gruel. He crouched over Annie, using his back to try to shield her from additional falling debris.

Dust rose in roiling clouds that choked lungs and burned eyes even more than before. In the distance, he could hear the rapid clanging of bells, meaning that some fire equipment was still in service and gallant crews were responding to the columns of smoke he could see starting to rise at all four points of the compass.

"Dear God, what do You want me to do?" Michael prayed fervently. "It'll take too long to carry her up Nob Hill through all this."

Casting around for answers, he noticed a group of loose horses. Five heavy-bodied work animals were congregated around one of the bubbling waterholes that had so recently appeared in the middle of the street. One of those horses, a huge gelding with a roached mane and braided tail, was wearing a harness that bore the fire department insignia.

Michael whistled. The dappled gray's ears perked up. It turned toward the shrill sound, then slowly began to approach, head down, the damp, dusty hide of its withers quivering.

The escaped fire horse was far too tall to mount while bearing his semiconscious burden, so Michael took hold of its halter and led it over to a fallen column. He wouldn't have tried to ride most other horses without a proper saddle but he knew this one, and as far as he was concerned it might as well have been heaven-sent.

Climbing up on the fluted edges of the stonework, Michael eased a groggy Annie onto the horse first, then swung a leg over so he could sit behind and keep her from sliding off. She moaned without totally regaining her senses.

Michael paused, his loyalties torn. Since his station had no teams and no usable equipment, there was little he could do other than proceed to try to ascertain where he and his fellows would be needed, as he'd originally been ordered. However, he'd also been told that he was free to use his own discretion so he would first ride to the Clark estate, deliver Annie and inquire about his mother and Tess.

If they were safe there, as he hoped, he'd be able to relax and return to try to find the chief or to simply concentrate on rescue work. If Tess was missing amid all this terrible wreckage, however, he wouldn't stop searching until he found her.

His heart would not let him.

* * *

Tess was passing the bay windows in the parlor when she caught a flash of movement out of the corner of her eye and saw a figure on horseback drawing nearer.

Far from prepared, she nevertheless hurried to the front door and threw it open, expecting to welcome the first of the refugees. Her jaw gaped when she recognized who had actually arrived.

Tess's hand flew to her throat where she felt her pulse fluttering madly. It was *Michael!* And he'd brought Annie home. *Praise God!*

"I'm glad to see that this house stood," he said by way of terse greeting. "Are you all right?" His voice sounded so hoarse Tess barely recognized it.

"Yes. Fine. And so is your mother. I just left her." She hurriedly approached. "What's happened to Annie?"

"I don't know. She's been pretty groggy." He scooted back so he could lift the young woman more easily and lower her to the ground. "Come and take her. I have to be getting back."

Tess held out both hands.

Michael eased his burden down.

Annie immediately recovered enough to begin to cling to Tess, sobbing quietly as if she were an injured child seeking comfort in the arms of its mother.

"Where did you find her?" Tess asked him.

He slid to the ground beside the horse and grasped its bridle as he answered, "She found me. Near Union Square. She fainted before she could tell me if you had been with her."

"Why would I be with her? You knew I was going home after the opera last night."

"I assumed so, yes, but I'd heard that a lot of nabobs did stay late to party at the Palace with Caruso. If she hadn't called your name before she fainted, I wouldn't have been confused."

"I sent her visiting in the city last night because I wasn't going to need her here. Her mother's house is on Geary Street, not far from where you say you found her." Tess managed a smile. "*Your* mother is busy cooking up a storm in case we need to take people in."

He took a few steps closer. "Good. I'm surprised to hear you still have enough gas for the stove. Don't count on it for long, or telephones or electricity, either. And guard your use of water till we see how bad that damage was. I suspect most of the mains are gone."

"All right." She continued to gaze at him with affection, hoping he would understand how much she cared. "Be careful? Please?"

"I will." The way his penetrating gaze met hers reminded her of the night before, only with even more empathy and concern. She yearned to reach for his hand but managed to restrain herself. Barely. "How bad is it down there?"

"Worst I've ever seen or ever hope to see," Michael said soberly. "A lot of buildings are either already down or soon will be. I know there can't be much left of Chinatown or the shacks along the waterfront, either."

"That's terrible. Wait. Why aren't you fighting fires?"

Averting his face, he seemed to concentrate unduly on

patting the horse's neck. When he did speak again, Tess understood why he had looked away. He'd been hiding the depth of his emotions.

"I was off duty, sleeping, when the quake hit," Michael said. "It's a wonder I survived. The whole station is in ruins."

"What about the other men?" Her heart ached for him, especially after he told her about finding his fellow fireman in the collapsed stable.

"I could just as easily have been the one staying down there with the horses," he added. "O'Neill made the choice to work all night because I'd let him sleep off a hangover earlier in the day."

That was more poignancy than Tess could resist. Keeping one arm around the still-weeping Annie, she grasped Michael's hand. "I'm so sorry."

"Thanks." He gave her fingers a quick squeeze before releasing them and starting to back the horse away. "I'm going to stop by the kitchen before I go. I want Ma to see for herself that I'm okay, in case she hears rumors about the station."

"Of course. Have her give you food and water. Take more than you think you'll need," she called after him as he walked away. "I'll tend to Annie."

Before Tess could finish shepherding her maid through the front door, however, the young woman dug in her heels. "No! I have to go back."

"Whatever for? It's dangerous down there. You heard what Michael said."

Annie was adamant. "I don't care. I couldn't find

my mother anywhere. The whole house fell down on top of us." Half sobbing, half hysterical, she gasped for breath. "You have to help me, Tess. We can't just leave her there. What if she's still alive and waiting for me to dig her out?"

Tess was ashamed that she hadn't thought that far ahead, hadn't considered Rose Dugan's welfare. Of course Annie was frantic. Any good daughter would be. Apparently, the disaster had rattled Tess's brain more than she'd first imagined or she would have remembered to ask about Annie's mother immediately.

"Do you think you can manage another trip this soon?" Tess asked, her heart aching for her friend.

"I can do anything for Mama."

"Then we'll go. Together. Just let me gather some supplies." She guided Annie into the house with an arm around her shoulders. "You go tell Mary to pack us a big basket of food, then have one of the men harness my mare to the smallest buggy. I'll go upstairs and collect sheets for bandages."

"I looked and looked and called for her as soon as I crawled out," the young woman insisted with a tremulous voice. "She didn't answer me. I couldn't find her anywhere. Not anywhere."

"Don't worry. We'll find her," Tess promised boldly.

In her heart, she was praying fervently that Annie's beloved mother was still alive. Judging by the indications she'd had so far, a great many people were not going to survive to see today's sunset over the Pacific.

* * *

Michael was just bidding his mother a fond farewell when Annie burst into the kitchen. Her hair was still ratted and her face streaked with dirt and tears. To his chagrin she was behaving irrationally, hurrying around the room and throwing food into a basket without bothering to even wrap it in a napkin.

He was about to tell her that he already had all the supplies he needed when she suddenly froze, covered her face with her hands and began to sob.

"There, there," Mary said soothingly, taking the young woman in her arms and patting her back. "You'll be all right. Sit down while I make you a nice cup of tea."

"No!" Annie pushed her away. "I have to go back to my mama's. I have to help her."

"Oh, darlin'," Mary crooned. "You can't be goin' down there all alone again. It's too dangerous."

Sniffling, the maid swiped at her tears and shook her head. "I'm not going alone. Tess is going with me. I have to get the buggy ready." She broke away and dashed toward the back door, brushing past Michael as if he were invisible.

Watching through the open door, Michael saw her race toward the carriage house. His heart sank. Until a moment ago, he had thought the situation couldn't possibly get any worse. Now, he knew better.

Giving his mother a peck on the cheek, he turned to leave.

"Are ye goin' back to work?" Mary asked.

"In a manner of speaking. The first thing I need to do is stop Tess."

Mary snorted. "Oh? And how do ye propose to do that?"

"I'll reason with her. Tell her how bad it is down below. She'll have to listen."

"Will she now? I'd like to see that."

"What else can I do? It's bedlam out there."

"I don't know. But giving that hardheaded girl orders isn't the way to go about it. You'd have a better chance of standin' on the tracks in front of a steam engine and expecting to hold back the train with your bare hands."

That opinion was so accurate it made Michael smile. He nodded. "I'll think of something."

By the time Tess reached the stables and joined Annie, there was a horse hitched to a buggy all right, but it wasn't her faithful mare.

She stopped, hands fisted on her hips, and stared at Michael. "What do you think you're doing?"

"Helping you get back to Annie's mother's safely," he replied, standing tall and showing no sign of being cowed by her display of righteous indignation.

"I'm taking my own horse," Tess insisted. "Unhitch your animal immediately."

Michael was slowly shaking his head as he held the gray gelding's bridle and led it a few paces, then fiddled with the length of the trace chains before he looked back at her. "No," he said flatly. "This horse is used to noise and strange smells. He's far less likely to bolt."

"My mare is fine."

"Here, she may be. And even that's not certain. Drive her by the worst of the damage and she's bound to smell death or fire and start to act up."

"Don't be ridiculous." In the back of Tess's mind she could see Michael's point but a rebellious tendency kept her from admitting as much. She stood her ground. "Well? I'm waiting. Remove your horse this instant."

"If I do—and I don't promise I will—how long do you think it will take you and Annie to get your mare into harness in his place? Do you have that much time to waste? Or should you stop arguing and get in the buggy so we can all be on our way?"

Tess felt Annie grab her arm and hold so tight it pained her.

"Please," the maid pleaded, "let's just go. You can argue with Michael all you want after we find my mama."

Although it went against her personal preference, Tess had to agree. "All right. Get in. I'm driving."

Instead of offering his hand and assisting her to climb into the buggy as he had in the past, Michael leaped into the driver's seat and took up the lines.

Tess pulled herself up and tried to shove him aside with no success. "Move over, sir."

"I think not," he said, giving her one of those grins that always used to curl her toes.

In this case, however, Tess seemed immune to his

Irish charms. Disgusted, she plunked down on the seat next to him while Annie climbed into the back to ride amid their provisions.

Tess kept her arms crossed and her spine rigid until they pulled out onto the road and started down the hill. She had to give up and grab hold when the buggy began to zigzag around piles of fallen masonry and bump over ridges of buckled cobblestones.

Thankful that Michael was driving, she watched him expertly squeeze the rig through newly narrowed passages and past hazard after hazard as they traversed the normally broad, open streets.

What she beheld was horrendous beyond words. Horses lay on their sides, unmoving though still in harness. Buggies and wagons were smashed. Whole city blocks of row houses had been reduced to matchsticks or were leaning so precariously they looked as if the slightest push would send them tumbling down one after the other.

Then, as Tess observed more and more of the damage and heard survivors keening over the bodies of the dead and dying, she wilted. Tears blurred her vision. Awe and fear filled her heart.

One hand gripped the side of the seat, her knuckles white from the sheer force of her grasp.

When she opened her mouth to speak, her voice was tremulous. "Oh, dear God," she said prayerfully, "help these poor people."

Beside her, she sensed the intensity emanating from Michael. It wasn't only the muscle power he was employing to handle the nervous horse amid such chaos, it was far more. His entire persona was as tight as a drum, his large, capable hands fisting the reins as if they were about to be snatched from him by a malevolence beyond imagining.

Tess could finally understand what he had been trying to tell her back at the house. This devastation was beyond human comprehension. Looking at what was left of the once-familiar streets and neighborhoods, Tess wondered how anyone, anywhere, could have survived.

Chapter Eleven

Michael would have done almost anything to keep Tess and her maid from having to view all this carnage but since they had insisted on coming, he figured it was best if he stayed with them as long as possible.

He had originally thought that the screaming during and immediately after the quake had been the worst part. Now that he was back in the thick of it, however, he realized that the murmuring, moaning and pockets of eerie silence could be just as bad.

Some men, women and children roamed the littered streets as if in a daze, barely cognizant of their surroundings while others were already lugging trunks and other belongings down the streets toward the railway station, the docks or the ferry terminals.

"You should have turned back there," Tess said, pointing. "Mrs. Dugan lives on Geary Street."

"We can't get through that way," Michael replied. "I tried earlier. Whole teams and wagons are buried under deep piles of rubble. The drivers are probably trapped beneath tons of bricks, too."

"Oh, my."

"That's not all," Michael went on. "Look over there. See all those loose wires hanging down?"

"Yes. Why?"

"Because they may be very dangerous, depending on whether they're electric, telegraph or telephone lines." He cast her a sober glance, meaning it to serve as a warning. Instead, she grasped his arm and held tight.

"Then you will be in terrible danger. How will all the rescuers manage?"

"I don't know. Let's take one crisis at a time," Michael said. It was his fervent hope that they'd quickly locate Annie's mother so he could be on his way again. He wasn't ready to think further ahead than that. The prospects were too demoralizing.

He carefully maneuvered the buggy through the rubble as far as possible, then stopped and climbed down. "Come with me. We'll go the rest of the way on foot."

"But what about Father's rig? If I abandon it he'll be furious."

"Suit yourself." Michael was already starting to unhitch his horse. "If I were him, I'd be more concerned about my family. Where was he this morning, anyway? I didn't notice him when I was at the house."

"Your mother said he took some of the servants and went to check his bank. He takes that responsibility very seriously."

"Ah, so that's why he wasn't underfoot giving orders. I wondered why we didn't hear him bellowing when you decided to make this trek."

"He would have understood. He might even have come along to help us."

Although Michael strongly doubted that Gerald Bell Clark was that altruistic he chose to keep his opinion to himself. So far Tess seemed to be going along with his sensible suggestions pretty amiably and the last thing he wanted to do was antagonize her.

Continuing to unhitch while his passengers retrieved cargo, Michael quickly led the horse out from between the shafts and tied up the long driving reins so they wouldn't foul or drag. He fastened a few bundles of their meager supplies to the horse's harness as Tess handed them to him.

"Are you sure Father's rig will be all right here?" she asked, hefting one of the picnic baskets Mary had prepared for them and leaning to one side for balance as she carried it.

Michael almost laughed at her naïveté. "Look around you. Do you think something like that really matters?"

"No," she said, sighing poignantly. "I suppose it doesn't." She looked to Annie. "I can't quite tell where we are. Is your mother's house close by?"

"Yes. Follow me," Annie said, taking the lead by stepping over more rubble in the street and wending her way west.

Finally, she paused and pointed. "There it is. See? The gray house with the porch that's fallen into the street."

Foreboding gripped Michael. Could anyone have lived through the crashing force of that building's collapse?

Sure, Annie had survived—and so had most of the other firemen who'd been asleep in the station house with him this morning, so he figured anything was possible. It just wasn't very likely.

"Where were you when it happened?" Tess asked Annie.

"Sleeping. Mama made me a pallet in the parlor."

That was apparently the portion of the home that was partially propped up on broken, misplaced rafters, Michael noted. The rear section, however, lay nearly flat on the ground.

He led the horse as close as he could, then hitched it to a lamppost, hoping it wouldn't run off if more tremors occurred.

Tess and Annie were already approaching the tumble-down house. Michael caught up to them.

"I was right there," Annie said, pointing with a trembling finger. "See? There's the corner of the gray blanket I was sleeping on."

"Where was your mother's room?" he asked.

Annie stared, wide-eyed. "Over there. Under the part of the roof that's on the ground."

"All right. We'll move as much loose lumber as we can and see if we can tell anything. If we still can't, we'll hitch the horse to the main rafters to pull them off. There's no other way we can possibly budge anything that big ourselves."

"But what if Mrs. Dugan is trapped under there?" Tess asked, grabbing his arm and halting him. "We can't move too much until we're sure we won't be hurting her."

It was an effort for him to ignore Tess's touch even though the sleeve of his shirt lay between them. "One decision at a time," Michael said, pulling away. "You two start over there nearer the street. I'll take this section because of the heavier timbers."

To his relief, both women hiked their long skirts to their boot tops and waded into the debris without further questioning of his authority.

When he heard Tess say, "Come on, Annie. I'll pass the pieces to you and you can toss them into the street," he wondered if she knew why he had assigned the tasks the way he had. Perhaps. He wanted to be the one to clear this section because he was relatively certain that Annie's mother lay beneath it. He couldn't protect the poor girl from the loss of a loved one but he could at least soften the initial blow by not letting Annie be the one to uncover the remains.

Tess was giving him a telling, sidelong glance and she nodded slightly when he looked over at her. She *did* know. And she, too, was trying to protect Annie. In spite of the dire circumstances, that conclusion warmed Michael's heart and made him proud. Not everyone who preached equality practiced it. Tess did both.

Tess's long, loose tresses were not only getting caught on the refuse as she labored, the hair that lay draped over her neck and shoulders was making her beastly hot. She drew the back of her wrist across her forehead to sweep away perspiration, hoping her face wasn't half as gritty as it felt.

Straightening to stretch her aching back, she sniffed something odd on the air. There was the usual scent of the ocean, as well as odors from countless other unpleasant sources, but this was different. This was far worse.

She glanced at Annie and saw that the girl was also wide-eyed with concern. What about Michael?

"Hey!" Tess shouted over at him. "Do you smell smoke?"

He whirled. "Yes. Get out of here."

Instead, Tess hurried to his side by stepping on what was left of the porch roof. "No. Let us help you."

"You can't do anything. Look." He pointed to puffs of smoke starting to rise from what was left of a nearby building. "It's liable to be too late in a few minutes. That fire's close and the wind's blowing this way."

Annie covered her face with her apron and began to sob hysterically while Tess tore at the remaining broken boards that still covered the area where Rose Dugan had lain.

"Go get my horse and back him in here," Michael shouted, grabbing Tess's shoulders and giving her a turn and a push to start her in the right direction. "We can't delay any longer."

"What if Annie's mother is alive under there?"

"Then we'll get her out, God willing. We can't leave her to burn to death."

"Where's the fire department? Why don't they come?"

"The stations that weren't destroyed have to be fighting

as many fires as they can handle already," Michael said, gritting his teeth and grabbing another armload of splintered wood. "Hurry up with that horse."

Tess couldn't fault the overwhelmed and undersupplied professional firemen who were risking their lives to try to save what was left of the city. She simply hoped and prayed that her meager efforts would be sufficient to help rescue the tiny sliver of suffering humanity that was currently relying upon the three of them.

"Dear God," she murmured, directing her plea heavenward as she tugged on the bridle of the stalwart fire horse and urged it to enter the field of splintered boards, "Show us where to look? Where to pull? Please?"

No booming, divine voice echoed from the sky but Tess nevertheless felt a sudden sense of peace and surety.

She turned the animal, gathered the harness traces and passed them to Michael, then watched as he fastened the ends around the nearest heavy beam.

The makeshift rig was ready in seconds. It was now or never.

Michael signaled and shouted, "Pull!"

Tess gritted her teeth, hiked a handful of skirt, grasped the horse's reins just below the bit and pulled as she shouted, "Git up! Go!"

The big gray leaned into the task, his muscles bunching, the leading edges of his wide front hooves digging in.

At first, nothing budged. Then she felt the load he was hauling give way and shift. He edged forward.

Afraid to look back, almost afraid to breathe, Tess continued to lead him slowly away, step by cautious step.

When she heard Michael shout, "Stop! I see her!" with such evident passion and exuberance, she whirled and stared. "Is she…?"

"She's alive," he yelled. "She's moving!"

Overcome, Tess leaned against the horse's neck and began to silently thank God.

Annie helped her mother crawl out from under her bed and Michael swung Rose into his arms so she wouldn't have to try to walk through the rubble.

"Are you all right?" he asked.

The older woman was both weeping and grinning as she clung to her daughter's hand. "Fine, fine." She cast a fond look at Annie. "I knew you'd find me."

"Tess helped," Annie said. "And Michael. I couldn't have done it without them."

"Then thank you. All of you," Rose said, half sobbing.

Michael was pleased to see that the older woman seemed to be in good condition, especially considering the fact that she'd had half a house sitting on her for several hours.

Tess was apparently just as surprised as he was because she quickly joined them to share a hug with Annie and ask, "What happened? How did she survive?"

Michael answered, "The old, solid oak bed she slept in supported the rafters enough that they didn't bear down on her. She's scratched and bruised but otherwise every bit as well as she claims to be."

"Prayers were answered," Tess said.

"Amen to that." They had reached the horse and he paused with his burden while Tess took its bridle to lead. "We'll hitch up the wagon again. I want you all to go to a refugee center and get checked out," Michael said, concentrating on Tess. "Mrs. Dugan needs to see a doctor and you may have injured your hands when you were digging."

"I agree about the doctor for Rose," Tess said. "But Annie and I are fine." Her brow knit. "I don't suppose she'll want to leave her mother, though. I can understand that. If my own were still alive I'd want to be with her."

"Good. Then it's settled. I'll carry Mrs. Dugan back to the buggy so she can ride while you lead the horse to keep him calm. Can you manage that?"

"Yes, but I should be getting home," Tess said.

To Michael's ears she didn't sound nearly as convinced as she usually did when she made a declaration like that. "Why? Your father may not come back for days. Not if he's as worried about the money in his bank as you think he is. Besides, my mother knows where you went and why. If Mr. Clark asks, she can assure him that you're fine."

"Am I fine?" Tess asked softly.

It concerned him to hear less and less strength in her speech, to see the sparkle leave her beautiful green eyes.

Clearly, she was exhausted yet unwilling to admit how weary she was.

"You will be," Michael told her. He was relieved to note that the Clarks' buggy was right where they'd abandoned it. The only things missing were a few household items from the back that they hadn't taken with them.

He placed Rose Dugan gently on the seat and assisted Annie aboard so she could sit close to her mother and steady her. Tess had already backed the horse between the shafts and was starting to hitch it to the tugs and breeching straps when he finished getting the others settled.

"Here, let me do that," Michael said, rushing to her aid. "You're tired."

"I may be tired but I'm not helpless," Tess insisted.

He might have backed off then, if he hadn't seen her trembling and sensed how close she was to losing control of her emotions.

Instead, he took those dainty hands in his and gently held them still. "I will never think that of you. This ordeal has been a terrible strain on everyone. If you won't rest for your own sake, do it for Annie and Rose. You need to be strong to look after them."

"I'll manage."

"I know you will." He turned slightly so Tess could see past him. "Look at their house. Even if Rose isn't badly injured she may be too upset to function. They'll need someone who is both intelligent and levelheaded. They'll need you."

He smiled, wishing their circumstances were different

so he could take Tess in his arms and comfort her the way Annie and Rose were comforting each other.

To Michael's delight, a wan smile began to lift the corners of Tess's mouth. She nodded. "I do understand. You're saying that this is only the beginning of our trials, aren't you?"

"Yes."

When she raised tear-filled eyes to him, sighed and took a step closer, he gave in and opened his arms to embrace her.

Tess slipped her arms around his waist and laid her cheek against his chest.

There they stood, out in the open in full view of what was left of San Francisco, and Michael didn't care a whit what anyone else thought. The only thing he really dreaded was the next few moments when he knew he'd have to force himself to leave her. How could he act nonchalant when he was dying inside at the mere thought of it?

Tess seemed to sense his emotional withdrawal because she leaned away enough to look up at him. "What will you do now? You said your station was destroyed. Where will you go to work?"

"I'm not sure yet," Michael replied. "I was on my way to find Chief Sullivan and get new orders for Station #4 when Annie waylaid me. He's a good man. If anyone can coordinate this fight and win it, Dennis Sullivan can."

"I saw a lot of water running down the streets," Tess said. "Will there be enough left in the main lines to put out the fires?"

"I don't know." Michael gazed into her lovely face, ignoring the smudges on her cheeks and the tangles in her flyaway hair.

Sadly, he understood far more about what was happening than Tess did. He might never see her again. Might never have another chance to bend lower and kiss her.

Even if she slapped his face for taking such liberties it would be worth it to try, he decided. Then if he had to enter eternity this very day, he could do so remembering the sweet taste of her lips.

He gently threaded his fingers through her long hair and cradled the back of her head. She was staring at him as if she yearned for what he was about to do. At least he thought so.

Slowly, as if handling fragile porcelain, Michael canted his head to the side and felt her arms tightening around his waist.

The brush of her warm, soft lips against his sent a shock wave through him like lightning arcing over the bay during a violent storm. His emotions became the ocean waves, his heart the pounding surf.

He sensed Tess rising on tiptoe to prolong their kiss, deepening and intensifying it until they were both left breathless.

When he finally set her away by grasping her shoulders, he could tell that she was every bit as staggered, as overcome with emotion, as he was. "I'm…"

Tess reached up and pressed her fingertips over his

mouth to silence him. "Don't spoil it by saying you're sorry, Michael. Please don't."

He kissed the fingers caressing his lips then grasped her wrist and placed a second kiss in her palm before closing her hand. "There. Keep that one for whenever you feel lonely."

"I am always lonely when you're not with me," Tess said, unshed tears glistening.

Afraid to reply for fear he might disgrace himself by weeping openly, he put an arm around her shoulders and ushered her closer to where the horse waited.

He bunched the reins before handing them to her. "There was quite a gathering of refugees in Union Square but I think it would be wiser for you to press on as far as Golden Gate Park to be farther from danger. Wait for me there. I'll find you."

"When?" Tess whispered. "How soon?"

"I don't know."

Placing one more quick kiss on her lips, he whirled and loped off, dreading the incontrovertible fact that his life might be required of him that very day and he might never again lay eyes on the woman he loved.

He already ached for her, for the precious moment they had just shared and for the days and years that lay ahead. If God took him in the line of duty, how would she cope with that loss? For that matter if something happened to Tess while he was otherwise occupied fighting fires or taking part in rescue operations, how could he ever forgive himself?

His eyes burned. His throat was raw. With tears

coursing down his cheeks and clouds of smothering smoke making him cough and gasp for air, he increased his pace.

At that instant, he wasn't sure whether he was running toward his duty or away from the overwhelming urge to give in and return to Tess while he still could.

Chapter Twelve

If Tess had not kept thinking about Michael and their all-too-brief kiss, she might have found it harder to cope with the sights and sounds and smells surrounding her.

Seated in the buggy, Annie and Rose clung to each other while Tess led the horse carefully, slowly through the ruins of the city and headed toward the enormous, rectangular park that lay between Fulton Street and Lincoln Way.

A pall still hung over the populace, although many people seemed to be snapping out of it. Here and there she actually heard laughter and spied children running and playing despite what had occurred. Youngsters were the most resilient survivors, of course, because they didn't truly comprehend the enormity of such a widespread disaster.

Tess could understand the intense emotional conflict the adults were experiencing. Part of her wanted to break down and sob while another part urged her to smile and perhaps even celebrate life.

There were many unfortunate souls who could not rejoice in their circumstances the way she and her companions could, and those people were to be pitied. However, even the worst losses couldn't negate the thankfulness of personal endurance and survival. To deny being grateful for that would be like questioning God's sovereignty.

There was a newly built decorative stone wall around the northeast corner of Golden Gate Park. Bypassing that, Tess worked her way into the park proper and stopped the buggy beneath the arching branches of a slim eucalyptus.

Quite a few larger, more substantial trees, such as cypress and pines, had actually been toppled by the quake, making her glad she hadn't been parked under any of them then. Nor would she take such a chance with those that remained upright—or with the monuments honoring President Garfield, Francis Scott Key and others.

Tying the reins loosely around the trunk of the sapling, she gave the trusty horse a pat and returned to her passengers.

"I think we'd better use the buggy to stake out our space," Tess said, "before so many others arrive that we're all jammed in together and have no privacy." Studying the gathering multitude and fearing the worst, she pressed her lips together.

"Will we be safe here?" Annie asked as she jumped to the ground and reached back with Tess to assist her mother.

"I think so. If there are too many more shocks we can always move over to the tennis courts. Since we have no idea how long we'll have to stay here, I think grass will make the best carpet."

"What about finding a doctor for Mama?" the maid asked.

"I'll see to that. You two stay here and guard our supplies while I scout around."

"Alone?" Annie's eyes widened. "You can't just go wandering off by yourself. What would your papa say?"

"Hopefully, he'd realize that I have a brain of my own and know how to use it," Tess replied, managing a smile. Now that they were ensconced among survivors and no longer had to keep looking upon the death and mayhem that lay beyond the boundaries of the park, she was feeling a definite sense of relief.

Little wonder that sounds of happy conversation and more playful children were so prevalent here, Tess thought. Although this situation was no cause for celebration it was, nonetheless, plenty of reason to give thanks. They were alive and well. And many thousands of other citizens were sharing that blessing, as well.

Given the alternative, it was perfectly natural to be joyous. After all, the worst was probably over and as soon as the firemen doused the fires they could all begin to restore life as it had been mere hours before.

Looking around her, Tess was struck by the uplifting sense of camaraderie and shared experience. Praise be to God they had found and rescued Annie's mother and knew that Michael's was safe and sound atop Nob Hill.

Other than Michael, whom she would always worry about no matter what, that left only her father to cause her a bit of concern. It was foolish to worry much about her father. Gerald Clark knew most of the important men in town as well as in state government, thanks to his financial status. If he had a problem, he could always call upon the mayor or even the troops that were stationed at the Presidio.

But Michael? Now that was a different story. Pausing, Tess scanned her surroundings, shaded her eyes and peered into the distance. Little smoke was visible to the north where the sea entered the bay. The Pacific shore lay down the hill, directly to the west, and the bulk of the bay was east, past the city proper.

What's left of the city, that is, she reflected, once again lamenting the terrible loss of life.

Papa would be more concerned with damage to property, of course, and she could see marvelous chances for him to eventually put some of his money to good use rebuilding the city he loved.

They could even open their home to refugees the way he'd suggested, she added, pondering possible ways to provide hot meals without endangering the house by lighting cooking fires before the chimneys were properly inspected.

Dodging wagons and pedestrians, Tess quickened her steps. She would first check the nearby clubhouse to see if there was medical assistance available inside. If not, perhaps someone there would be able to direct her to a doctor for Rose.

Thinking of the older woman's narrow escape made bile rise in Tess's throat. If they had been a few minutes later, Annie's mother would surely have burned to death in the splintered ruins of her home.

"And if I hadn't listened to Michael and let him use *his* horse, we would probably have arrived too late to save the poor woman."

That sobering thought settled in Tess's heart and mind like a boulder. Michael again. Always Michael.

A sudden yearning to be with the gallant fireman filled her so thoroughly she felt dizzy. A nearby slatted wooden bench offered temporary respite and she quickly availed herself of it.

Seated with her elbows on her knees, her hands pressed over her face, she closed her eyes and began to pray for the man she loved, focusing more than she'd ever thought possible and shedding silent tears for the life she feared they might never have a chance to share.

For Michael, the trek to the fire station on Bush Street seemed to take forever. When he arrived and saw the pile of bricks from the collapsed chimney of the California Hotel lying atop the smashed firehouse, he gaped, then grabbed the arm of the nearest passing fireman and insisted on being informed of the station's status.

"There ain't no station, if that's what you're meanin'."

"What about the chief engineer? Where's he?"

"On his way to the hospital, if any of 'em are still standing. Sullivan's quarters collapsed with him and his wife inside. She's okay but the chief fell all the way through to the basement and ended up scalded by a ruptured steam pipe from the boiler. He's alive but it don't look good."

"Then who's in charge?"

"Beats me. Battalion Chief Walters said that we should just stand by till he decides what to do. He said he was gonna drive around and see what was going on if he could get his buggy through these streets. And I ain't seen hide nor hair of acting Chief Dougherty since before the quake."

"What about survivors? Who's helping them?"

"Don't know. You volunteerin'?"

"Could be. I know where there's a spare horse and buggy we could use." Michael hesitated and clapped the young man on the shoulder. "Will you be all right?"

"I ain't never gonna be all right again and that's a fact." The dusty fireman shook his head and wiped his sooty eyes. "Maybe this is Armageddon."

"I don't think so," Michael said, "but time will tell. If we get more shakes, be sure you and the others are in the clear." He eyed what was left of the once-thriving California Hotel. "There are still enough bricks hanging on up there to do plenty more harm if they fall."

"Don't know that I care much at this point," the young man said. "Seems unfair for the best chief we ever had to die right when we need him the most."

"I thought you said he was still alive."

"I did. But I saw the burns and I wouldn't wish sufferin' like that on my worst enemy. He ain't gonna make it. No way."

"That's up to the Almighty," Michael said.

Snorting, he wiped his nose with his sleeve. "This shouldn't of happened. No, sir."

Michael had no ready rebuttal because he didn't understand, either. No one could. If the earth had trembled a few hours earlier he would have been the one tending to the horses and he might easily have been killed instead of poor O'Neill.

His breath caught. What if the quake had come while Tess was still at the opera? He hadn't seen the edifice himself but he'd heard that it was in shambles. The loss of life the evening before, when Caruso had been performing for a packed house, would have been catastrophic. Those who had not been killed outright would probably have been trampled to death by others who were trying to escape.

The notion that Tess could have been caught in that tempest of human agony cut him to the core.

"But she wasn't. She's safe," he reminded himself firmly. "And I have work to do."

His mind was spinning. Where to begin without proper leadership? Who was going to take over and manage the manpower and equipment the various departments had left? He didn't have the rank or authority to do so no matter how much he wished he could.

Until Battalion Chief Walters returned or acting Chief Dougherty instituted some kind of overall battle plan, it looked as if he was as much on his own as the gangs of men who were wandering the streets and stopping to pull survivors from the wreckage at random.

That was a worthy goal, at least for now, Michael decided. Speaking to the fireman he'd just encouraged, he explained, "Union Square is filled to overflowing. I'm going to go get a wagon and start hauling the injured and elderly over to Golden Gate Park. When Walters or Dougherty get here, tell them Company D only lost one man that we know of, but we have no usable equipment. We'll need a new assignment."

"All right. If I see 'em I will. Who knows whether Walters'll even make it back?"

"He has to," Michael insisted, looking into the distance and seeing clouds of billowing smoke and a telltale reddish glow. "If somebody doesn't take charge soon we could lose the whole city."

The other man gave a guttural laugh. "If you ask me, she's already a goner. We got no communication, no alarm system, and half the hydrants are dry. Cisterns the same way. The ones that've got water are so full of garbage they're 'bout useless, or so I hear."

"All we can do is make the best of whatever we have," Michael said. "I'll stop by later and see if there's any plan of action yet."

And in the meantime, he told himself as he turned and started to jog toward the park, *I'll be able to check on Tess again when I commandeer her rig.*

He knew there were plenty of other conveyances he could appropriate but he wasn't about to do so. No, sir. Not when this plan included seeing his beloved Tess once more.

Chapter Thirteen

By the time Gerald Bell Clark reached his still-erect bank building, Phineas Edgerton was already there looking after things.

"Phineas! Good man. How bad is it?"

"Bad enough, G.B. Have you seen the crowds in the streets? Rabble. Pure rabble. No telling what they'll do in these circumstances. Maybe even storm the vault."

"My thoughts exactly," Gerald said, patting the younger man on his slim shoulder. "I brought extra men with me and stationed them outside to act as guards. And we have plenty of ammunition. I think we can hold off a small army, if it comes to that."

"What about your house, your daughter?"

"Tess will be fine. I ordered her to stay home."

Phineas huffed. "What makes you think she will abide by your wishes when she's been filling her head with all that woman suffrage nonsense?"

"My daughter is a reasonable person. She'll do as I say. And she'll eventually agree that you are the best choice for a husband, too. Just give me time. I'll bring her around."

As Gerald watched, he saw the other man's expression harden. Not that he could blame him. Tess was a headstrong woman, one worthy of being a Clark, yet difficult to handle.

Gerald was certain that his choice of Phineas as his future son-in-law would prevail, even if it took Tess a little time to accept the idea. The man was a gem, unfortunately not too muscular or particularly comely but with the intelligence and shrewd instincts a successful banker needed. And once Tess became his wife, the Clarks and the Edgertons could merge their fortunes and create a banking dynasty that was unrivaled. It was a perfect plan.

Eyeing Phineas, Gerald stifled a grimace. His grandchildren might turn out to be gaunt-looking with long, hooked noses if they didn't happen to favor Tess's side of the family tree, but that was the least of his concerns. Once he got her married off and properly settled, he could stop losing sleep over the possibility of her making a poor choice of a husband and start fully concentrating on his business again.

Gaining that kind of peace of mind was worth any sacrifice. He should know. He'd made a similar one when he'd married the sickly but wealthy wife who had borne him a headstrong, troublesome daughter instead of the strapping son he'd always wanted.

As Tess wended her way through the mass of refugees she was both amazed and befuddled. Many were sooty and weary but others seemed so nonchalant about the circumstances that had forced them out of their homes it was incomprehensible.

Well-dressed women in fancy frocks, coats and the kind of elaborate hats she and Annie had worn to the suffragette lectures were chatting, laughing and holding sway as if they were about to serve tea in their own drawing rooms. Many had apparently had some of their finest furniture transported to the park so they would be comfortable there, acting as if they considered the outing a mere lark. Didn't they know about all the poor souls who had perished? Didn't they care?

"All right," a man shouted just to her right. "Everybody smile. Let's show those hoity-toity easterners that nothing bothers us here in Frisco."

Tess paused and scowled at him. He had a tripod and small camera set up and was actually taking photographs in the park, apparently bent on taking full advantage of the disaster to fill his pockets with filthy lucre. And he wasn't the only one. There were pushcarts brimming with fruit and baked goods making the rounds. Even the Chinese had come, apparently for safety as well as to peddle their wares, and were freely mingling with residents of the city who would normally have treated them with disdain.

Still, wasn't this the kind of equality and freedom Maud Younger had espoused? Tess wondered. *Perhaps,* she answered, *but what a shame it took such carnage to bring it about.*

Reaching the small clubhouse where she had expected

to find some semblance of organization, Tess was greeted by a group of rowdies instead of the refined gentlemen she had expected. The crudely clad young men had taken over the main room as if they belonged there and were in various states of repose. Some had even propped their muddy boots on the manager's desk with no apparent qualms.

Tess hesitated briefly before deciding that she was being too quick to judge. After all, she was anything but pristine-looking herself, having dressed without much thought and having later employed her bare hands to dig through the wreckage of Rose's house.

She nervously brushed her palms over her skirt, tossed locks of her long hair back over her shoulders and cleared her throat. "Excuse me. Can any of you tell me where I might find a doctor?"

The raucous laughter that ensued told her she had been right to prejudge these men, fair or not.

"You want *what?*" one of them asked, shouting to be heard above his cronies' catcalls.

"A doctor. I have a friend who may be injured."

He snorted and spat onto the already filthy floor. "Lady, are you crazy? There ain't no docs here and there ain't gonna be. Go on now. Leave us in peace."

"But…"

One of the other men lobbed a juicy apple core toward the doorway. It splatted on the floor, just missing the hem of Tess's skirt.

Startled, she jumped away, to the amusement of the

entire group, then whirled and began to run back toward the spot where she'd left the horse and buggy.

Why had she let Michael convince her to come here? They should have gone home, to the house on Nob Hill, where they'd at least have had a roof over their heads and sufficient food and water.

Suddenly realizing she'd become disoriented, Tess stopped and turned in a circle. Everything looked different than it had just minutes ago. Tides of people were entering the open grounds in a never-ending flow of humanity, evidently bringing with them as many of their worldly goods as they could carry. A few were even towing chairs with bundles lashed to their seats in lieu of a suitable wagon or cart.

Seeking to find a landmark and get her bearings again she stood on tiptoe. All she could see in the distance was the same surging, jostling, pushing, determined kind of horde that surrounded her.

Outside the park boundaries a steady procession of erstwhile evacuees rushed by, headed for the docks or to the railway station although Tess couldn't imagine that those tracks were in any better shape than the buckled remains of the trolley routes that had been thrust out of the ground like so many twisted jackstraws.

As she turned back to scan the park grounds, the head of a familiar-looking gray horse rose above the hats of men and women in the distance. Tess's jaw gaped. She stared. Someone was driving her buggy toward her, against the main flow of pedestrian traffic. No one had permission to take her rig. Therefore, a thief must be making off with their only means of transportation!

Hiking her skirt to her shoe tops, she began to elbow, shoulder and zigzag her way through the crowd as best she could. "Excuse me. Let me through. Please, move aside. I must get past."

Time slowed. She felt as if she were taking one step back for every two she took forward. People pushed her. Blocked her without seeming to even notice. Impeded her progress until she was ready to scream.

She refused to give up. Surrounded closely by the swarm of people, she could no longer actually see the horse's approach but she remembered that it had been headed for the gateway she had finally reached. *Praise God.*

Panting to catch her breath and coughing from the smoky air, she waited while trying again to peek over the heads and hats that kept interfering with her view.

The horse suddenly burst through as the crowd parted and gave ground. Tess lunged for its bridle and grabbed a fistful of reins below its bit, shouting, "Stop! Thief!"

Startled, the animal tossed its head, nearly lifting her off the ground. She held tight. Her sharp cry of, "Stop this buggy this instant," seemed to have the desired effect because the command was obeyed.

Ready to shout for a policeman or at least appeal to passersby to assist her in exacting justice, Tess gritted her teeth, stepped to one side of the heavily muscled horse's chest and looked up, ready to give the driver a good scolding.

Her jaw dropped. *Michael?*

The fight went out of her as quickly as her breath had and she sagged against the animal's neck, overcome with gratitude to her heavenly Father for bringing them together again in spite of the turmoil.

Michael was beside her in a heartbeat, taking her in his arms and consoling her. "Calm down. It's just me. You're all right."

All right? Oh, yes. She was more than all right. She was superb.

Her own arms slipped around his waist. She knew she should say something, do something, but for those few precious moments all she wanted was to stay precisely where she was. With him. With her Michael. As long as he was willing to hold her close and comfort her, she was more than delighted to let him do so.

"I have to borrow the horse and buggy," he said, lightly kissing the top of her head and noting how satiny her lovely hair felt in spite of its tangles. "I knew you wouldn't mind. Most of the buildings in the city aren't safe. I'm going to be bringing in the folks who want to come here and can't make it on their own." His grip tightened for a moment before he released her. "Can you get back to Annie and Mrs. Dugan by yourself?"

He could tell Tess wanted to say no, but she nodded affirmatively instead. That was like her. She might be barely able to drag one foot after the other, yet she'd insist she was fine.

"I'll make sure I come by to check on you as often as I can," he said. "I promise."

She gazed up at him. "What about the fires? They must be bad. We can see a lot of smoke from here. Look at this air. I hurts to take a deep breath."

"I know." Michael wasn't sure how much to tell her, then decided that knowing the truth was better than believing the wild rumors that were undoubtedly circulating.

"Chief Dennis Sullivan, the man I was counting on to manage this battle, was mortally injured in the quake," he said, watching her reaction and seeing the empathy he knew she'd express.

"I'm so sorry."

"We all are. It's my understanding that some of the alarms are being repaired but so far there's no real organization. Fires are burning around Market and Kearney, and of course on Geary Street where the Dugans' house was."

"There must be more than that," Tess said, gripping his forearm and blinking back tears. "I know I see signs in other places."

He noted the passage of the bright silk robes of a group of Chinese: men, women and children as well as two-wheeled carts of trade goods and personal possessions. "Aye. I expect Chinatown to be leveled, if it isn't already. Those shacks are like a tinderbox just waiting for the strike of a match."

Michael knew it was wrong to delay any longer when he was sorely needed for the rescue efforts. Tearing himself away from Tess was going to be one of the hard-est things he'd ever had to do.

"I have to go," he said tenderly as he pried her fingers from his arm. "I have work to do."

"I know." Wide-eyed, she stared up at him. "I can't just sit here and bide my time when I may be able to help, too. Take me with you."

"That's out of the question." He was about to turn away when she grabbed his shoulder.

"No! Wait. I have a wonderful idea. There are more horses and buggies in our stables. If we head that direc-tion I can hitch up a much bigger rig and we can either each drive one or I can ride with you. What do you say?"

His initial reaction was denial. Then he gave her idea more thought and had to agree that portions of it had merit, though it was also fraught with danger.

"How do you propose to get a larger buggy like the cabriolet through these streets?" he asked. "Chances are good it will break down before we've gone a block. What then?"

Facing him, Tess fisted her hands on her hips. "That rig you're driving is the most fragile of them all and you know it. Papa has an old freight wagon at home. It's sturdy oak, with wire-rimmed wheels. If we hitch a four horse team and put your sensible, strong one in the wheel position for stopping power on the hills, we should be fine. And we'll be able to haul a lot more, too."

"That makes sense," Michael finally said. "Give me a note so your grooms know I have permission and I'll do it." He could tell before he'd finished speaking that his alteration of her proposal was not going to meet with her approval. Not even slightly.

"Oh, no, you don't," Tess said with a lopsided smile. "I'm not going to make it easy for you to get away from me this time. If you get orders to go fight fires I won't argue, but until that time I'm going to become your shadow."

"You are a stubborn, willful woman, Miss Clark. Do you know that?"

"I certainly do," Tess replied. Her grin spread. "Now, are you going to stand there and debate or are you going to drive me back to see Annie so I can tell her where I'm going?"

Without ceremony he hustled her to the buggy, spanned her small waist with his hands and lifted her high enough to place her feet inside while she shrieked the way she used to when they had played and teased as children.

Her eyes were bright, her cheeks flaming when she plopped down onto the seat, slid over and watched him climb aboard.

Michael took up the reins. So far, he'd had no problem with anyone trying to usurp their transportation but he knew that was probably only because those fleeing the city were not yet desperate enough to begin acting like an unruly mob. That kind of behavior would start soon, he feared. Which was another reason why he'd have preferred that Tess stay with the Dugans and that everyone remain inside the park. There they'd be safe from possible aftershocks, spreading fires and anticipated threats of violence.

He cast her a sidelong glance and found himself admiring her fortitude immensely. She was an extraordinary person, one he was privileged to know. That she was a comely *woman,* even with her long hair hanging loose and her cheeks smudged, did not escape him either. Nor would it escape the notice of the city's criminals when the usual rule of law was overturned due to a lack of ready enforcers.

Once they reached the Clark estate, Michael vowed, he was going to do more than change wagons. He was going to arm himself so he could defend Tess's honor. That was an added reason to keep her close by, he rationalized. As long as she was with him she'd be even safer than if he'd left her alone with the others in the park.

His justification wasn't really logical. He knew that. He also knew he considered it providential that he had encountered Tess at all. If it hadn't been for the tall, stalwart fire horse standing out above most of the crowd he'd have had a terrible time locating Annie and Rose in the first place. His disappointment when Tess had not been with them had been palpable.

That was when he'd begun praying to see her again. And soon after that she'd run up to him and accused him of theft. Given the slim chances of that meeting amidst all this chaos, he had to assume that his fervent prayers had been answered.

Transferring both driving lines to his left, he took her hand in his right and held it gently. "It will be worse out there every time you go. People are hurt and dying. So are animals. Are you sure you're up to this?"

When she threaded her slim fingers between his, smiled and said, "I can do anything if I'm with you," Michael was immediately so filled with joy he felt shamefaced. It seemed wrong to experience happiness when so many were suffering. Yet when Tess was by his side, how could he possibly feel otherwise?

Chapter Fourteen

During the tortuous drive back to Nob Hill, Tess tried to focus on how she'd help others rather than dwell on the dire situations she couldn't hope to alleviate. So much misery. So much loss. If she opened her mind to the vast hopelessness all around her she was afraid she wouldn't be able to function at all, let alone make herself useful.

Michael guided the buggy past the impressive Crocker and Huntington estates, then turned up the drive of the house she had called home for her entire life. It was good to see how little damage the stone-clad mansion had sustained, although it did show thin cracks radiating out from the corners of a few of the tallest windows gracing the drawing room and her father's library.

Mary was waiting on the stoop next to the kitchen door, wiping her hands on her apron, when Tess climbed down and embraced her.

"You brought her back." Mary looked lovingly at her son. "Bless you."

"We're not staying," Michael said. "Tess will explain. I'm going to the stables to water this horse and change rigs. While I do that, you two start packing up more bandages and supplies."

"Of course."

Tess could see unshed tears brimming in the older woman's eyes and she realized there was moisture in hers, too. She normally wasn't one to weep so easily. Apparently, the sight of so much suffering had brought many people to the edge of their endurance, including her.

She whisked the telltale dampness off her cheeks as she led the way into the kitchen. Mary had managed to lay out a grand spread of food on the table as if expecting guests.

"Have many people stopped by to eat?" Tess asked.

"Only your father and a few of the servants, so far. Mister Gerald said he left some of the men watching his bank and was going to drive around in his motorcar looking for more to hire as guards."

"You did tell him where I'd gone, didn't you?"

The look of pity on the cook's face told Tess what had happened. Regardless, she chose to ask, "He didn't even miss me, did he?"

"He was just preoccupied with other things," Mary alibied. "I'm sure he figured you were right here with me, like you are now."

"Well, I'm not staying," Tess said firmly. "I'm going back down the hill with Michael."

"Mercy, no!" Mary's hands worried the apron into a

knot. "You can't be doin' that. Not with everybody in such a tizzy. 'Tis safer here."

"Nevertheless, I intend to help all I can. Michael needs me. I'm going to be there for him."

"Is he daft?" She grasped Tess's shoulders. "Think, girl. What if you're attacked? There's always a bad element by those docks. No tellin' what they'll get up to once they see there's no law."

"I've thought of that. So has Michael. I promised to fetch Father's pistols and a box of bullets. We won't be going back unarmed."

Mary began to wring her hands and weep. "You can't do that. I've heard shooting. And terrible explosions."

"That's just the authorities clearing a path so the fire can't progress. Michael heard that Mayor Schmitz and General Funston decided to use dynamite to make a firebreak around the mint."

"What about all the gunshots? How can you hope to hold your own if there's so much lawlessness?"

"Most of that firing was probably from the army," Tess said. "The mayor himself told the soldiers to shoot looters on sight." She patted the cook's hands. "Don't worry on our account. Michael knows all the firemen and most of the police by sight, if not by name. We'll be fine."

Squaring her shoulders and wiping her eyes with the corner of her apron, Mary regained control. "Well, then, don't just stand there, girl. Go fetch those pistols while I pack you some more food."

Tess paused just long enough to plant a kiss on the

older woman's damp cheek, then turned and raced up the stairs to her boudoir. She grabbed a carpet bag from the armoire and quickly stuffed it with extra articles of clothing and toiletries she thought she might need.

Pausing to scan her room and think, she was about to head down to the library to raid her father's gun cabinet when she remembered her mother's journal.

Before she could change her mind, she slid a hand beneath her bed pillows and retrieved the slim, ribbon-tied volume. It went into the carpetbag with her clothes. Then, she wheeled and ran.

With no handy helpers left at the Clark estate, it took Michael nearly fifteen minutes to find suitable harnessing for the rest of the team he was assembling. He was finishing preparing the fourth horse when Tess joined him.

"Good choices," she said, tossing her bag and some bedding into the wagon bed while Mary added sacks of food before returning to the kitchen for more.

"Put big Jake, the roan, in the other wheel position," Tess said, "and I'll hitch my mare in front of him."

"I couldn't find any tack here that would begin to span the girth of the gray," Michael replied. "It's a good thing he already had most of his fire department rig on when I found him running loose."

"Father prefers lighter, faster teams, as you can tell."

"Where is he?" Michael asked, dreading the possibility that Gerald Clark might venture outside and accost them.

Tess's sharp "Ha!" told him otherwise. "Papa is off tending his money, as usual," she said. "He's so concerned about me he didn't even remember to ask after my welfare when he came home to get his automobile."

"Just as well." Michael chanced a grin in the hopes it would lift her spirits. "I'd hate to have to explain why I was making off with his horses, his wagon *and* his daughter." To his relief, Tess smiled.

"Plus the brace of ivory-handled pistols in my carpetbag," she said. "I think he'd be more concerned about getting those guns and his rig back, especially if we were taking the cabriolet. I seriously doubt he'll miss this wagon. Or me."

"That's another good reason to stay with me. I missed you so badly this morning I almost gave up my job just to come looking for you."

"I know you'd never really do that," she said, gazing at him so sweetly his heart nearly melted. "But I do thank you for the kind thought."

Quickly convincing himself that he needed to double-check the traces on her side, Michael ducked under the chins of the two leading horses to bring himself closer to Tess before he spoke from the heart. "What you said when I saw you after the opera was right. We do need to have a private talk. When this is all over there are some important things to discuss." Emboldened by the tender look in her eyes he grasped both her hands.

Without any comment other than a slight smile, Tess

tilted up her face, closed her eyes, stood on tiptoe and brushed a kiss across his lips.

It was barely a breath, like the warm summer breezes that sometimes drifted over the hills toward the sea, yet it touched him so deeply he could hardly think, let alone find the rest of the words he wanted to speak.

He knew this was not the right time to confess his love for Tess, no matter how badly he wanted to. Delaying their return to the city for any reason could cost innocent lives. Thinking only of themselves was not the proper way for good Christians—or anyone else, for that matter—to behave.

Michael bent to return her kiss and lingered mere moments before he steeled himself to face his duty and whispered, "We need to go."

It seemed to Tess that the more needy people they stopped and picked up, the more they encountered waiting by the side of the road and begging for a lift. The wagon bed was already filled to overflowing, plus there were able-bodied men walking alongside while their women and children rode.

Tess was thankful that Michael's temporary assignment was to rescue and gather the living because they had passed many other wagons, and even a few automobiles, that were being used to haul away the dead. Those sights were so ghastly and shocking they turned her stomach.

He halted the team when they came upon another fireman in uniform. The man was bending over his buggy.

Judging by the way its body was canted, the axel had snapped.

Michael called to him. "Chief Walters? Is that you?"

The man straightened. "Aye. Mahoney?"

"Yes, sir." Michael saluted. "I've been looking for you. Any orders?"

"Not yet. I've checked on all the stations. It's bad. Don't know what we'll do without Sullivan."

"Is he still alive?"

"Yes. They transferred him to the Presidio but it doesn't look good."

Tess noted that the older fireman was eyeing their loaded wagon. "Looks like you found a way to make yourself useful. Keep it up for now. By tomorrow morning we should have a better idea about what we'll need. If you can get to Union Square and it's still open, report to me there at eight. If not, go down to the ferry terminal. We've got men and equipment coming over from Oakland and San Mateo then, too."

"Why wait till morning?" Michael asked.

Walters's shoulders sagged and he sighed. "Because they've got their own problems over there. It's the same all up and down the coast. Only they don't have nearly the fires we do." He shook his head. "Never thought I'd see the likes of this day."

"How many men have we lost?" Michael asked. "The only one I know about is O'Neill, from my station."

"A couple of others, far as I know. And some police officers. I haven't even tried to get an accurate count yet."

When he took out a handkerchief and blew his nose, Tess could tell it was mostly to mask his raw emotions.

While Michael bid the chief goodbye, Tess spotted two barefoot children standing across the littered street. She hailed them. "Do you two want a ride to the park so you don't hurt your feet on all this glass and trash? That's where we're going."

Their grimy faces brightened and they headed for the wagon as if they had just been offered a piece of cake.

Tess scooted as close to Michael as she possibly could to make room for the slim, dark-haired girl and her little brother on the driver's seat and greeted each of them with a hug. "Are your parents nearby? Might they need a lift, too?"

Both children lowered their heads and stopped looking at her. The girl murmured, "No, ma'am," and began to weep as she pointed to an immense pile of rubble.

"I'm so sorry," Tess said. "You can stay with me and my friends for now, if you want. We have a nice place saved in the park." She paused and smiled. "My name is Tess. What's yours?"

The girl was the only one who looked up. "I'm Rachel and this is my brother, David."

"Pleased to meet you." Tess turned to Michael. "I think it's time we headed for the park and unloaded these folks so we can come back and start again, don't you?"

"Yes. I just hate to leave anyone behind."

She saw him eyeing the horizons and assumed he was sizing up the conflagrations that still threatened the heart of the city as well as some outlying areas. Every direction she looked there was more smoke, more ominous glow, more signs that the situation was growing worse.

Distant explosions continued to startle her as well as the horses, and although Michael seemed as stalwart as ever, he had nevertheless armed himself with one of her father's pistols, leaving the second one for her.

Resting her hand lightly on the back of his, she sought to reassure him. "You're doing all you can right now. The chief just said so."

"I know. But that doesn't make it any easier to wait patiently when I've been trained to fight fires."

Pondering what else she could say that might ease Michael's mind, Tess was distracted by a tiny movement beneath the edge of a broken board at the side of the road. It might be nothing, yet she was positive she'd spied something odd.

An intense compulsion to investigate made her grasp Michael's arm and shout, "Stop!"

He tensed. "What's wrong?"

"Over there. I thought I saw something."

"What?"

"I'm not sure." She was already clambering past the youngsters and climbing down from the wagon on her own. "I'll be right back."

Her initial loud exclamation had startled the horses and Michael was still having to work to control the team, so she knew he wouldn't dare follow. That was just as well. With all the horrible things they'd come upon already, there was a fair chance her imagination was playing tricks on her. She almost hoped that was the case.

Tess slowly, warily, approached the pile of wreckage that had drawn her attention. Whatever had originally caught her eye wasn't visible from this angle. Pausing, she listened intently. A soft mewling was coming from beneath a nearby splintered board. A kitten, perhaps?

Taking cautious steps, she bent to lift the slab of wood and was astonished to uncover a pudgy little blonde girl. The child looked barely old enough to walk. Her blue eyes blinked open. The moment she saw Tess hovering over her she puckered up and began to wail.

Tess waved to the crowd at the wagon. "Over here! Somebody help me look."

She quickly scooped up the wailing toddler, held her close and stood back while several of the men from the wagon and a few hearty passersby began to throw aside heavier wreckage in that immediate vicinity.

It took only seconds to uncover two bodies. One was a young woman who was clutching a baby blanket as if she had been trying to flee to safety with her child. Next to her lay a once-handsome man who had likely died assisting his wife and baby.

Saddened, Tess carried the probable orphan back to the wagon where helping hands pulled them both aboard. Women crowded around to coo and sympathize and admire her newfound treasure. So did Rachel and little David.

"Is the baby okay?" Michael asked.

"I don't see any injuries. I think she's upset because I scared her, that's all."

"Well, there's sure nothing wrong with her lungs."

The men who had left the group of refugees to help Tess search were returning to their families. Someone in the rear of the wagon passed forward a small quilt and Tess wrapped the tiny girl in it, cradling and rocking her in spite of her loud lamenting.

"Hush, baby, hush," she cooed. "We'll take good care of you. I promise." She rocked more. "Hush, now. That's a good girl."

When she finally raised her gaze from the child to look at Michael again, the expression on his face was so touching, so heartrending, it brought unshed tears to her eyes.

She assumed he was thinking the same thing she was. If only they had driven through this particular area sooner, had thought to look here before the baby's parents had succumbed, perhaps they could have saved the whole family. But they had not.

Tess kept reminding herself that the waif she was cuddling and trying to comfort had survived the collapse of an entire apartment house. That alone was a wonderment. Finding her parents alive and well, amid all that horrible wreckage, would have been next to impossible no matter how soon they or anyone else had begun to search.

She followed Michael's line of sight past her shoulder and watched as other men continued to pull bodies from the rubble of the tenement and lay them out in the street.

All over the city, piles of the dead were growing. How many there would be when the final tally was made was beyond imagining.

Moved beyond words, Tess pressed the child closer and continued to rock her. The little girl's sobbing lessened. She chanced a peek by lifting a corner of the coverlet and saw that the precious, exhausted little one had not only fallen asleep, her breathing had grown more natural.

Closing her own eyes, Tess prayed wordlessly for the child's lost parents and for all the others who had gone to glory already. How long would it be before rescuers like Michael and his comrades had the opportunity to rest, let alone sleep? The way things looked at present, it was going to be a long, long time.

Michael halted the loaded wagon in an open area near where the Dugan women were camped. "Okay," he announced to his passengers. "This is as far as I go. Be sure you take all your things with you when you leave."

He paused by the front wheel to lift the brother and sister down. He tousled the boy's mop of hair, then pointed the children to the Dugan camp before helping Tess disembark.

"I'm going to take this baby to Rose and Annie for temporary safekeeping," she said. "They'll know how best to care for her." A slight smile lifted the corners of her mouth. "I'm afraid my education as a nurse for children is sadly lacking."

"Looks to me like you're doing fine. Is she still asleep?"

"Yes. I keep checking her because I can't help but worry. I'll feel better when Rose has had a good look at her, too."

"Okay. Hurry back. We'll need to be heading out again as soon as possible."

"I will. Don't leave without me."

The sight of Tess cradling the tiny tot as she turned and started to walk away reminded Michael of a Christmas crèche. She'd make a wonderful mother some day. Experienced or not, she was nurturing and loving the same way his mother was. Tess's strong will and decisiveness, in addition to those other sterling qualities, would stand her in good stead no matter what trials life presented.

Trials such as these, Michael concluded, taking in the multitude that had already begun to raise makeshift tents in the park and settle into a semblance of routine and order.

There were myriad kettles warming over small fires or portable kerosene stoves and the like. Families were resting together on pallets composed of blankets and whatever other suitable materials they could assemble. If it hadn't been for the foggy air, the smell of smoke and the booming of dynamite that shook the ground as badly as some of the aftershocks had, the encampment would have seemed like nothing more than a bunch of city folks enjoying leisurely afternoon picnics in the park.

Frowning as he finished emptying the wagon of

passengers and their household goods, Michael started to look around for Tess. Why hadn't she returned? What was taking her so long?

Concerned, he climbed aboard the wagon for added elevation and scanned the crowd, starting with the eucalyptus sapling which marked the Dugan encampment. There was Annie. And her mother was bending and talking to the two youngsters they'd just delivered.

In the extra moments it took him to also locate Tess, Michael's heart began to pound. Perspiration dotted his brow. Then, he spotted her reddish hair and his breath whooshed out audibly.

Relief was short-lived. Tess wasn't alone with Annie, Rose and the children. Someone else was with them. Even from that distance, the man's bowler, cane, tailored suit and foppish mannerisms looked decidedly familiar. And most unwelcome.

Rather than leave the wagon to approach on foot and chance actually losing their only means of transportation to thieves the way Tess had imagined, Michael maneuvered the team closer.

He halted them directly behind the dandy in the black bowler hat and wrapped the driving lines around the brake handle.

Judging by the man's uneasy stance and the way Tess was facing him with her hands on her hips, Michael was fairly certain she was not pleased. Then he heard her order, "Go away, Phineas," and was positive.

Jumping down, fists clenched, Michael came at the other man from the rear. Tess's glance and quick smile

telegraphed his approach, however, and he lost the element of surprise.

The banker whirled and raised his silver-handled cane
defensively. Instant recognition registered in his narrowed eyes. "What do *you* want?"

Michael stood his ground. "I should be asking you
the same question."

"I've come to escort Miss Clark out of this disgusting
muddle, not that it's any of your business," Phineas said
with a jut of his chin that emphasized disdain.

"I'm making it my business," Michael countered.
"Miss Clark has chosen to stay here with me, and I'll
thank you to stop bothering her."

If the situation hadn't been so serious he would have
laughed aloud at the air of dismay and astonishment on
the banker's weasel-like face.

The man looked to Tess, apparently realized she was
in full agreement and snapped his jaw shut.

She began to grin. "There you have it, Mr. Edgerton.
Now, if you'll excuse us, we have work to do. Please
assure my father that I am in very good hands."

Circling Phineas while he stood there looking at her
as if she had just fed him unsweetened lemonade and
then punched him in the stomach besides, Tess offered
her hand to Michael and let him help her climb back
aboard the freight wagon.

As Michael joined her, took up the lines and urged the
team forward, she slipped her hand through the crook
of his elbow and snuggled closer, much to his delight.

Tess giggled softly, privately. "At least you didn't have

to threaten to shoot him, although a good scare like that might have served him right."

"Don't tempt me."

He knew his grin was far too satisfied to be respectful but he couldn't help himself. These trying circumstances were painful in many ways, yet they had also brought him closer to Tess than he'd ever hoped to be. Even after the danger was past and the city returned to normal, he'd remember these hours with both sadness and jubilation.

Every person they rescued was one more sign that life went on; and every loss, like the tot's parents, was a reminder of how precious each day should be.

It wasn't that Michael didn't realize how desperate their overall situation was or how much worse it could still become before it was over. He was simply doing the only sensible thing by taking one minute, one hour, one day at a time.

What the future might bring was more than unknown. It was almost too frightening to ponder.

Casting a sidelong glance at his lovely companion as they drove out of the park, he prayed, *No matter what becomes of me, Father, please look after Tess. She is the dearest thing in the world. I know I don't deserve her. Please take care of her and help her find the kind of happiness she's earned.*

The idea that he might not be a part of Tess's future, might not be granted further blessings regarding the woman he loved so intensely, so completely, haunted Michael's thoughts.

Wisely, he refused to dwell on such a possibility. Right now they both had vitally important work to do. If Tess had not been with him on the last trip, that poor babe might not have been discovered, might not have been rescued in time. That alone was proof he should let her continue to accompany him, at least for as long as he deemed it safe to do so.

The traffic in the damaged streets had lessened measurably, probably because many citizens had already fled. He imagined they didn't much care where they went as long as they were far from the shaking, although as Chief Walters had said, the earthquake had caused severe damage many, many miles away as well.

Thankfully, the electrical power plants had been shut down for safety's sake. So had the gas. Night would soon be upon them, leaving little light other than that from an occasional lantern and from the fires still raging in the distance.

"At dusk I'm going to take you back to the Dugans' and leave you there," he told Tess. When she stared at him and opened her mouth he quickly added, "Don't argue. I plan to go check in with Chief Walters again, assuming I can locate him in all this chaos, and see if I can persuade him to give me an assignment right away instead of waiting for morning."

"Meaning, you don't want me underfoot?"

"I wouldn't have put it quite that bluntly, but yes. It's my job."

"And you need to do it. I know how badly you want to."

Michael nodded and smiled wryly as he looked down

at the backs of the team. He and that big gray horse were a lot alike in their instincts, weren't they? Every time they heard the clanging of an engine in the distance or saw flames, they both tensed, both acted as if they wanted to forget everything else and race to the fire, which, of course, was exactly how they did feel.

It was Michael's most fervent wish that he could make Tess understand that fact when he finally had to leave her. This brief time they'd managed to spend together had already lasted longer than he'd dared hope. Sooner or later, they were going to have to part.

There was no other option.

Chapter Fifteen

Tess spent the bulk of that night dreaming she was still beside Michael, still thrilling to the sound of his voice, still safe and secure because of him and only him.

As she began to stir she found herself picturing his handsome, rugged face and remembering his expression when he'd finally bid her goodbye.

Tess could tell he hadn't wanted to leave. When he'd put his arms around her she'd simply stood within his embrace and relished every moment. Then, she'd lifted her face and he'd kissed her.

Seconds later, breathless, he had stepped back and apologized. "I'm sorry. I had no right to do that. Especially not in front of all these people."

Tess remembered smiling while also being afraid she might burst into tears. That was the last thing she wanted to do, particularly since an open expression of sorrow might have made their parting even harder on Michael.

"I suppose we could have hidden away behind a bush

or something to spoon, but don't you think that would have raised even more eyebrows?"

To her relief, he'd then began to give her the tilted, Irish grin that was his trademark. "Are you inviting me to misbehave, Miss Clark?"

"Not yet," she'd replied. "But don't lose hope. I soon may."

Michael had grasped both her hands then and held them tightly, forming both a barrier and a bridge between them as he'd said, "I look forward to it."

That was the moment Tess now remembered with the most fondness. It wasn't their actual parting that gave her shivers of nervous delight, it was the promise of a bright future. With Michael.

She sat up and rubbed her eyes. Explosions in the distance continued to shake the ground. Around her, much of the camp was stirring and she could smell the pleasant aromas of coffee and frying bacon.

Yawning, Tess saw Rose and Annie fussing over the baby while Rachel and David devoured enormous bowls of oatmeal as if they'd missed many meals and were trying to make up for it all at once.

She joined the other women. "How is our baby this morning?"

"Hungry," Rose said. "I was worried that she might be a finicky eater but that's not going to be a problem."

"Do we have enough food?" Tess asked, glancing at the older children. "If not, I can go home and get more from Mary."

"There's plenty," Annie said. "You should rest. You worked too hard yesterday."

"I can't argue with that," Tess said with a smile as she raised both arms over her head and tried to stretch some of the pain out of her muscles. "I am definitely not used to doing that much physical labor."

"I'd fetch you a cup of coffee but I don't want to stop tending the baby," Rose said. "Maybe Annie…?"

"Nonsense. I'm certainly capable of doing things like that myself." Tess tossed her head to swing her long hair back over her shoulders and leaned carefully over the fire to reach the pot. It wasn't familiar. "Where did you get this, anyway?"

"Scavenged it, right out in the street over there," Annie said proudly. "You'd be amazed at how much stuff is being thrown away as people head for the ferry. The streets are lined with piles of precious things."

"That was very smart of you," Tess said. "I was all over town yesterday and it never occurred to me to pick up a thing."

"It's not like I was looting," the maid insisted, coloring. "The pot and these cups were just lying there, abandoned on the ground. I rinsed them down by the lake before I brought them to Mama."

"And we're all glad you did."

Settling down and sipping her hot coffee, Tess gave thanks for many things, including the baby's health. The only clue anyone had to the child's name or family was of the tiny locket she wore and the approximate location in which she'd been found. It was hard to make out the faces in the pictures but Tess had high hopes those images would nevertheless help identify the child's surviving relatives and return her to what was left of her family once a proper system for doing so had been established. The same was true of the older children, although they were capable of giving their names so there would be no doubt.

Calling to Annie, she asked, "Is there anything I can do to help either of you?"

Since both women were quick to assure her there was not, Tess decided to try to make herself presentable, just in case Michael had a chance to return before reporting for fire duty.

She reached into the carpet bag for her hairbrush and felt its smooth tortoiseshell handle. At the same time her fingertips brushed the journal she'd grabbed on a whim. It had been wise to preserve it because it had belonged to her late mother, she assured herself, handling the slim volume as if it were a precious relic and wishing she'd thought to rescue the family Bible as well.

Should she untie the narrow pink satin ribbon and read her mother's private musings? Tess wondered. Surely, there was no reason not to. Not now. Not when Mama was gone to glory.

Tess cradled the book in her arms, pressing it against her chest, her heart. In the midst of this crisis she wished mightily that her mother was still beside her, still able to offer comfort and counsel. Since she was not, however, perhaps she had left behind some wise words which would help at a time like this.

Seating herself atop a pile of folded blankets, Tess untied the ribbon clasp and opened the book, laying it across her lap to peruse while she worked the tangles out of her long hair at the same time.

Mama's early years seemed pretty mundane, Tess noted, leafing through them quickly. Then as her mother adjusted to marriage and tried to please her husband, the mood subtly changed.

The rhythmic movement of the hairbrush stilled. Tess stared at the page she had just turned.

I have had a lovely baby girl, she read. *My Gerald is upset, of course, but he'll soften toward her eventually. I know he will. And I have promised that we shall try again for the son he covets so.*

Tess knew she shouldn't have been surprised to read such a plain truth because she had often heard her father say practically the same thing, yet it hurt to read that Mama had agonized over it, too.

There was more to follow, special mentions of Tess's babyhood accomplishments and her ensuing youth. The pages were filled with love and appreciation for her daughter but continued to lament the fact that there had been no additional son.

Flipping to the back of the book, Tess swept aside the blank pages until she reached one of the final entries.

I fear I shall not go to heaven, her mother wrote. *I harbor too much unforgiveness in my heart. I want to love my husband the way I used to but I cannot. I have tried to bear the son he wants and have failed him. Now it is too late. May God forgive me.*

Through her tears, Tess read one more line, its words directing her to turn the page. There, she saw a notation addressed to her!

My darling Tess, I hope you may someday see this. Don't weep for me. Weep for your father. He is a bitter, unhappy man and surely will remain so for as long as he lives. You were my best and only joy and I always loved you dearly. I pray that you will find the happiness I missed and that you will live the life of your dreams, not try to mold yourself to anyone else's desires.

Follow your heart. Read the scriptures as I taught you. And remember that I loved you more than life itself. It was signed, *Your loving Mama.*

A tear dropped, dampening the paper and causing the ink to start to bleed.

Tess quickly closed the book and dabbed at her eyes. "Poor Mama. And poor Papa, too," she added, realizing how her parents' lives had been at hopeless odds for so many years.

In retrospect she ached for her mother. Yet she could also see how that attitude of daily martyrdom might have caused her father to withdraw. Papa liked his world well-ordered. Within his control. Managed to the hilt. To have a wife who was not only ill but clearly disappointed in her entire existence when there wasn't a thing he could do about it must have driven him to distraction.

Sighing, Tess got to her feet and slipped the journal back into her carpet bag with the hairbrush. She tugged at the hem of the jacket of her wool dress and smoothed the outfit over her hips, dusting the skirt with her hands and shaking out the hem.

When this turmoil was past and they were back at home, she'd talk to her father, she vowed, and let him know she understood why he'd always seemed so gruff. That might not change anything between them but she felt beholden to try.

Beginning to smile wistfully, she looked out at the crowd and thought of Michael. There was no sign of him or of the team and wagon this morning so she assumed he had already reported to Chief Walters. That was the most likely scenario, although she couldn't help hoping he was currently on his way to the park with one last load of refugees, instead.

No matter what, Tess vowed to be ready. She ran her fingers over her hair to smooth it carefully, then once again patted at her dusty skirt.

She couldn't imagine anything else, now or ever, that would mean more to her than catching sight of Michael Mahoney and she wanted him to be just as pleased when he saw her even if she hadn't been able to change her clothing or have her long hair properly dressed.

She smiled, remembering the way he'd threaded his fingers through her loose tresses when he'd kissed her. Truth to tell, if there was the slightest chance he'd repeat that loving act she might never, ever, pile her hair atop her head again.

The sun shone bloodred as it began to peek through the smoke-filled atmosphere and add another kind of glow to the eastern sky. Michael had checked Union Square the night before and had seen nothing to indicate it would be a usable gathering place. Therefore, he planned to report to the ferry terminal. He had time for only one more task before he went on duty.

Walters's and Dougherty's decision to hold some able-bodied men in reserve made sense; he just kept wishing his station hadn't been destroyed in the initial earthquake so he and the others of his company could have gone to work immediately.

In the next hour or so, Michael intended to make certain his mother was safe no matter what. Judging by the position of the rising sun, it was still early, though the haze and smoke made it impossible to be certain of the time.

A strong wind had arisen at daybreak, made worse by the circular updraft the fires themselves were generating. Flames rose in death-dealing tornados, bearing millions of hot embers aloft then showering them over the roofs and other remains of previously unscathed buildings.

His jaw clenched. Crumbled relics of total destruction lay everywhere and buried among them many poor souls who had been unable to save themselves. Those were people he and his fellows should have been able to rescue. Somehow. That was what they'd trained for, stood ready for. Who could have imagined that the fire brigades would fall victim to so much devastation before they had a chance to even act?

The view from Nob Hill, once he reached it, was also disturbing. Michael called out to his mother as he stopped the team outside the mansion and was relieved when she burst out and ran straight into his arms.

"Oh, God be praised," Mary keened. "I didn't know what to do. The fire…"

"You're still safe here, at least for the time being. But I want you to pack up so I can take you down to the park to stay with Tess and the others."

"Why? Surely the firemen will stop this soon."

Michael shook his head slowly, considering the carnage he'd just passed. "I don't know when. None of us do. Mayor Schmitz has ordered blocks of buildings close to the fires blown to bits instead of trying to cut a firebreak farther away. That system doesn't seem to be working."

Mary gazed up at him, tears welling. "I promised Mister Gerald I'd stay and watch the house even if all the other servants left."

"Have you seen hide nor hair of him?"

"Nobody's been here since yesterday. Mr. Clark swore he was going to look after the money at his bank no matter what."

"That figures." Michael glanced up at the shimmering half disk of light peeking over Mount Diablo. "I have about an hour, by my reckoning, before I have to report to the ferry terminal. Go get your things and load all the food you can carry into sacks or pillowcases while I see if there's a decent horse left for you to ride." He gestured at the team. "These animals have done more than enough."

"But…"

Michael stood firm. "No buts, Ma. There's no time to argue."

As Mary turned away she paused long enough to ask, "Is Miss Tess all right? And our Annie and her ma?"

"They're fine. Now hurry."

It hadn't taken his mother's mention of Tess to bring her to Michael's mind. She'd never left his thoughts, his prayers. The aura of her natural beauty and her tender smile would dwell with him, in his heart and mind, forever and always.

And, God willing, he'd see her once more, at Golden Gate Park this very morning.

Tess was pacing and beginning to get terribly anxious when a slim dirt-dusted young man burst through the passing crowd and accosted her.

"Miss Clark!"

She frowned, puzzled, before recognizing him as a messenger boy her father had often employed. "Jimmy?"

"Aye. It's me." He snatched his soft tweed cap off his head and clutched it in grimy fingers.

"Did Papa send you?"

"No, ma'am. I come myself. He told us all to go away but he won't leave."

Tess touched his arm through the sleeve of his sooty shirt. "Is fire threatening the bank?"

The boy shook his head, his tousled hair scattering bits of ash and dirt. "Worse. It's the dynamite. A soldier said they was gonna blow up the whole block and we should clear out, but Mr. Clark, he won't budge."

Eyes wide, Tess scanned the distance. Smoke hid details of the city so well it was impossible to tell how close the danger might already be to her father.

"All right, Jimmy. You've done your duty. Now either go find your family, if you can, or stay here with us. Rose and Annie will give you something to eat and drink."

The youth looked worried. "Yes, ma'am. Thank you, Miss Clark." He squinted up at her. "You gonna go talk some sense into your papa?"

"If I can," Tess said. She pulled a shawl around her and stood tall, shoulders pinned back by determination. "Tell the others where I've gone. As soon as I've seen Father I'll come right back, one way or the other."

She heard him answer, "Yes, ma'am," as she strode off. It would have pleased her mightily to have Michael's moral and physical support at this moment but since he was probably already working, as he should be, she'd handle Papa alone.

Michael would be proud of her for taking initiative, she reasoned, and once she'd joined her father she'd also have the opportunity to convince him he truly was loved by poor Mama and also by the daughter he had never fully accepted.

That was one of the main reasons Tess felt she must make the trek to the bank. The Lord had used the journal to show her what she needed to do and say with regard to her father. If she tarried she might never get the chance to make things right between them.

* * *

Less than half an hour had passed when Michael arrived at Golden Gate Park with his mother. He'd asked a man with a pocket watch for the correct time and had been relieved to learn he was running ahead of schedule. That pleased him no end because it meant he'd be able to steal a few minutes of precious time with Tess before he had to leave her again.

Helping Mary dismount and shepherding her to the lean-to Annie had strung up from a bedsheet, he started to unload the sacks of provisions they'd had tied behind the saddle, handing them to the older children while he watched the women share mutual hugs and weep for joy.

The unloading completed, he placed the final bag on the ground and frowned. "Where's Tess?"

"She—she's gone," Annie said, clearly upset. "I would of stopped her if I'd known what she was planning. She was gone by the time the boy told me."

"Gone? Where? What boy?" Michael knew his tone was harsh and demanding but he didn't have time waste.

"To Mister Gerald's bank," the maid said. "A messenger told her the army was going to blow it up. She went to fetch her papa."

"Into *that?*" Michael swept his arm in a gesture that encompassed the destruction outside the park. "What was she thinking?"

Annie's compassionate tears and soft, sobbing reply failed to reach his ears or touch his heart. Turning on his heel, he mounted the fresh horse and made sure the pistol in his belt was secure. Then he yanked the reins to spin the horse in a tight circle, aimed it toward the gate and kicked it. Hard.

By his calculations he had little time left in which to locate Tess and see that she returned to the park, with or without the idiotically stubborn father who had caused her to leave the place of sanctuary.

"That's a laugh," Michael muttered in self-disgust. "Gerald Clark's hardheadedness can't hold a candle to his daughter's."

Chapter Sixteen

Panting and coughing, Tess wiped her smarting eyes in a futile attempt to stop them from burning. She blinked rapidly, hardly believing what lay before her. The street was not only eerily deserted by every single citizen, there wasn't an armed guard or a soldier apparent, either.

The only nearby action seemed to be taking place directly in front of Papa's bank. A familiar-looking figure was loading bulging canvas sacks into the back of what looked like a greengrocer's wagon and covering them with loose hay.

She approached with a frown. "Phineas?"

He didn't even deign to glance her way. "What do you want?"

"My father," Tess said. She looked in the direction of the bank's double doors, half expecting to see her predictable papa lugging more sacks of money toward the wagon. There was no one else in sight.

"Where is he?" Tess asked.

"How should I know? When I got back from running

errands for him he was gone." Snorting in obvious derision, Phineas began to cough and wheeze. "This smoke's
about to kill us all. I suggest you leave."

"Not until I find my father."

"Have it your way," the younger banker said snidely.
"Just stay out of my way."

"What are you doing?"

The look he shot her was clearly derisive and demean-
ing. "I should think that would be obvious, even to you.
I'm preserving your family fortune for you while your
dear father runs away to save his own skin."

Hardly, Tess thought, perusing her surroundings in
more detail and immediately spotting proof she was
right. Papa would never have left without taking the
fancy new automobile that was parked thirty feet away.
There were not enough of those expensive contraptions
around for her to be mistaken, particularly since he'd
had it painted a deep maroon instead of settling for the
usual black color.

Realizing that Phineas had been lying, she saw no
reason to stand around and argue, particularly since she'd
left the park in such a hurry she'd forgotten to bring one
of Papa's pistols along.

Tess quickly gathered her dusty skirts and lifted them
so she could more easily scale the piles of building stone
and decorative carving that had fallen from the façade
of the once-impressive building.

The bank's mahogany-framed doors, with gilded
lettering on their glass inserts, were standing ajar. She

stepped through the portal and stared, hardly able to believe her eyes.

Plaster had fallen from the ceiling and pieces of it were scattered across the previously highly polished marble floor of the lobby. More white flecks also dusted the bars enclosing the now-empty teller cages, making them look as if a snowstorm had recently occurred inside the bank.

"Papa?" Tess cupped her hands around her mouth and called again, louder. "Papa, where are you?"

Suddenly, the fine hairs on the back of her neck prickled and her skin began to crawl.

In an instant she knew why. A sinister voice vibrated in the stillness. "I told you he left. You should have listened to me."

Shivers shot up and down her spine. She held her breath. Phineas was standing directly behind her, so close his breath was palpable. His presence was not only frightening, it was clearly menacing.

Before she had a chance to whirl and confront him, he caught her upper arm in a painful grip and began to propel her toward the door to her father's private office.

Tess pummeled him with the fist of her free arm and tried to break free. "Let me go! What are you doing?"

"Just taking care of business like I told you," he replied. Jerking open the door to the office, he shoved her through.

She stumbled forward, nearly losing her balance. The immediate slam of the door made more plaster rain down. The ominous clicking of the lock gave her chills.

Recovering and growing angry, Tess peered into the dusty gloom, afraid of what she might see. There was a strange-looking dark shape lying at the far end of the oriental rug.

"Papa!" She ran to him. Fell to her knees at his side. Touched his shoulder. He didn't move.

Lather whitened the neck of Michael's horse. He thanked God he'd saddled a fresh mount from the Clark stables when he'd fed and watered the weary team and turned them out into a paddock.

The horse's shod hooves clattered on the cobblestones while Michael prayed the beast was as agile as it looked. This kind of speed was not only impulsive it was just plain reckless even on a good day, which this certainly was not.

As he neared the bank he could see something happening out in front. Although he wasn't particularly surprised to spy the dislikable dandy who pleased Gerald Clark so much, he wondered where the older man had gone. His fondest hope was that Tess had joined her father and that they were both safely away from the danger. Then he noticed Clark's abandoned motorcar and his heart sank.

Leaping off the horse before it had slid to a full stop, Michael grabbed Phineas by the shirtfront. "Where's Tess?"

"You're the one who said you were taking care of her. What's the matter? Did you lose her?"

"She said she was coming here," Michael shouted. "Now where is she?"

The wiry man didn't answer. Michael saw his beady eyes dart first to the bank doorway, then aside to the street where the automobile sat, then back to the bank. That was his answer! Tess was in the bank.

Michael flinched and ducked as an explosion less than a block away shook the ground and loosened even more of the bricks and stone that had not fallen in the original earthquake or its aftermath.

Casting his odious captive aside like useless rubbish, he raced into the bank. "Tess! Where are you? Answer me!"

A second explosion drowned out any reply there might have been and brought down a fresh rain of plaster.

Before that echo had died, Michael was already twisting the knob on the door that displayed her father's name and title. It didn't open.

"Tess!" He banged with his fists. "Tess, are you in there?"

"Yes! Look out for Phineas," she shouted. "He locked us up."

Michael whirled, expecting an attack. Instead, he saw the loaded wagon driving away with Phineas Edgerton holding the reins and cracking a whip over the backs of the team.

"Stand away from the door," Michael yelled, pausing only a second before he added, "Are you back?"

"Yes. Hurry!"

One swift kick with the flat of his boot was all it took to spring the latch and free the prisoners.

Tess immediately threw herself into his arms and clung tightly while her groggy father leaned against the jamb for support and mopped his brow.

The older man's head was bleeding slightly and he looked ashen but Michael was satisfied all would be well—until he heard G.B. order, "Get your hands off my daughter."

"No, Father, no." Tess continued to hold fast to her heroic fireman. "Michael is rescuing us. It was Phineas who locked us in."

"That's impossible. The Edgertons have impeccable breeding. One of theirs would never do such a thing. You've misunderstood. Phineas is merely helping me preserve the bank's funds."

Pointing to the now-empty street, Michael disagreed. "Oh, really? Then where is your wonderful vice president and where is your money?"

It should have gratified Michael to see the older man's shoulders droop as reality dawned. Instead, he actually felt sorry for him.

Gerald rubbed his sore scalp, noticed traces of blood and used the handkerchief to tend to the wound. "I thought another earthquake had knocked me out but now I wonder. I don't remember a thing after I walked into my office."

"He must have hit you from behind." Tess released her hold on Michael enough to give her father's arm a brief pat. "Come with us. I have a tidy little camp set up in the park. We'll look after you."

It was clear to Michael from the narrowing of the banker's eyes and the way he was staring into the street that he had no intention of letting Edgerton escape. In this terrible confusion, however, successfully following anyone would be next to impossible.

Placing a light kiss on the top of Tess's head, Michael sighed and delivered his own bad news. "I can't go with you, remember? I have to report this morning." He looked to the older man. "Will you take Tess back to the park?"

Although Clark's reply was neither quick nor firm, he finally nodded and said, "Yes."

Satisfied, Michael cupped Tess's face in his hands and tilted it up for one last kiss. He didn't care if her father had an apoplectic fit over it, he was going to bid the love of his life a proper goodbye.

His mouth was tender yet demanding, almost desperate, she noted, as if he feared that this might be their last touch, last kiss.

The emotional turmoil bubbling inside Tess brought to mind words she had not intended to speak—at least not until she and Michael had calmly discussed their mutual feelings. Her lips parted. Trembled. Looking directly into his eyes, she whispered, "I love you."

Moisture sparkled in the depths of his dark gaze. He froze and stared at her. "I…"

To Tess's dismay he never finished the sentence, never

told her he loved her in return. Instead, he whirled and strode away.

Michael's abrupt departure left her totally confused. How could he just walk off like that? Hadn't he heard what she'd said? Didn't he care? In her deepest heart she was certain he loved her, so why hadn't he spoken the words?

She felt her father's hand at her elbow. Blinking back tears, she managed a wan smile for his benefit.

"Come on," Gerald said. "I'll drive you back to the park in my automobile."

Tess could tell from his tone and posture that that was not at all what he wanted to do. "If I weren't here, would you go after Phineas instead?"

The older man shrugged, clearly disheartened. "I don't know. Perhaps."

"Then let's."

"Don't be ridiculous. You don't belong out on the streets in the middle of all this. Don't worry. I'll look after you." He smiled slightly. "After all, I did promise your young man."

"He is, you know. My young man, I mean," Tess said, blushing. "I know he's not highborn or rich, the way you wanted, but I love him dearly."

Blowing out a noisy sigh, Gerald nodded. "Well, I guess we can forget about you marrying Edgerton in any case." He wiped his brow and blotted his eyes with the crumpled handkerchief. "I can't believe how fooled I was. Thank goodness you didn't take to him the way I'd hoped you would."

Tess huffed. "I loathed that odious man from the first moment I met him."

"You did?"

"Yes. The things I learned at the suffragette meetings have helped me stand up for myself." She smiled when she saw her father's bewildered expression. "Don't look so shocked, Papa. All I mean is that I now trust in myself, know my own mind and stick to what I feel is right. That leaves Phineas out in the cold."

She laughed softly at the imagined image of the skinny, supercilious fop literally shivering from the cold shoulders she'd already given him. There was no man for her except Michael Mahoney and she knew it—all the way from the top of her head to her toes.

"Besides," Tess said, growing dreamy eyed as she pictured Michael, "I prefer gallant firemen."

"Is that what the young man does for a living?" Gerald asked. He cupped her elbow, gestured at the door and started to escort her toward his waiting motorcar. "He's Mary Mahoney's son, too, isn't he?"

"Yes, and I can't think of anyone I'd rather have for a mother-in-law."

"You two have discussed matrimony, then?"

Tess sobered. "No. Not yet. But we shall." She colored slightly. "I'm sure Michael will do the right thing and ask you for my hand."

"Let's hope so." Gerald brushed soot and ash off the upholstery on the automobile's passenger seat before assisting her into it, then walked to the front of the car to crank the starter.

Before he could bend to begin, Tess stopped him by adding, "I want to marry for love, Father. I don't want to count on it developing later, the way it did for you and Mama."

It was immediately clear, judging by the befuddled look on his face, that her conclusions had been correct. Her poor father had never viewed his marriage as a love match. She saw his lower lip quiver.

"It's true," Tess insisted before he could argue. "Mama loved you dearly. I read all about it in her journal."

He stared. Blinked rapidly. Took a deep, shuddering breath, then said simply, "Thank you."

This was the perfect moment to speak her mind, to tell him the rest of the things she'd planned to say. Nevertheless, Tess's pride and the memories of his past rejection almost stopped her—until she thought of how Jesus had always taught his followers to forgive.

Emboldened by her faith and the knowledge that what she was about to do and say was right, she added, "And *I* love you, too, Papa."

The changing expression on her father's lined, weary face was a combination of tenderness and awe. He was clearly thunderstruck, so much so that his jaw dropped.

Like Michael, he didn't choose to return her profession of affection but in this instance Tess was satisfied. Papa had loved Mama and he loved her, too, in his own way. Although he had never been a demonstrative man, he harbored deep feelings, feelings that now shone in his countenance.

That will do, she concluded, basking in a sense of familial belonging that she had never known before. Both her parents had done their best. The only truly sad thing was that Mama had passed on without knowing how much Papa had cared for her.

Tess vowed she would never allow that to happen with Michael. She would tell him every day how much she adored him. And he would hold her in his arms the way he had a few moments ago and…

A lump in her throat and a rapid pulse signaled the rise of the lingering fear she'd kept denying. Her last glimpse of Michael Mahoney might have been the final one she'd ever have. He was about to enter the belly of the beast, to stand and fight a fire that had already consumed a third of the city or more.

Given the terrible ongoing danger and the lack of proper tools with which to wage that battle in spite of the influx of engines and men from Oakland and other cities, he might not survive long enough to become her husband.

Chapter Seventeen

A portion of the fire had jumped Van Ness at California and Powell streets and was climbing the side of Nob Hill by the time Michael joined his fresh crew. They all donned leather helmets and heavy canvas coats.

"You're in charge of this team, Mahoney," Chief Walters ordered, gesturing at the horses hitched three abreast in front of the steam-powered pumper. "We don't know if there's any water left east of Van Ness but the navy has fireboats working the docks so I'm sending you and some of the others up Powell. Do the best you can. And God help you."

Michael nodded, his mouth dry, his nerves taut. He'd definitely done the right thing when he'd moved his mother out of the Clark mansion. It sounded as though they might soon lose their battle to preserve the expensive homes of the city's most affluent residents.

"That's no different than losing Rose Dugan's house," he muttered to himself, knowing he was right. Any person's home and possessions were valuable to them, no matter how little monetary investment was involved. Perhaps if the fire departments had had more ready equipment and manpower to wage war on this disaster in all areas of the city in the first place, the conflagration wouldn't have spread so far and gotten so out of hand. Then again, no one could possibly have foreseen a battle like this.

He climbed aboard the engine, set a booted foot on the brake and threaded the pairs of reins between his fingers so he could control each individual horse. The snorting, pawing, sweaty team was more than eager to be off.

"Ready, men?" Michael shouted back at his crew.

When he was answered with a chorus of affirmative shouts he snapped the reins, gave the horses their heads and braced himself as they lunged ahead, blowing hard and straining to get the heavy engine rolling.

Michael had little chance to do more than skillfully guide the team but he did manage to see, as they drew nearer to Nob Hill, that several mansions had already been reduced to smoldering ruins.

Above them the newly built but never opened Fairmont Hotel, which had been billed as the jewel of the city, was starting to look as if every window was brightly curtained in dancing, deadly orange and red.

He shouted to the horses. They kept up the frantic pace, the pumper careening left and right as they dodged debris littering the streets.

For the first time in the past few days Michael's mind was too occupied by the task at hand to return to thoughts of Tess more than occasionally. He was approaching a staging area where other engines and crews had massed to make a stand against the fire's progress.

"Whoa," he shouted to the team. "Whoa, boys. That's it. Easy, now."

Bringing his rig to a stop at the edge of the group, he called down, "Where do you want us?"

The chilling answer wasn't long in coming. A sooty, sweaty fireman looked up at him and shook his head sadly, somberly, his shoulders slumping as if he were on his last legs.

"I wish I knew," the man called back. "You boys might as well spit on that fire. We just ran out of water in the last cistern."

Tess sat beside her father as he drove cautiously toward the park. She could tell he was pondering something important because now and then his brow would furrow or his lips would form a grimace.

"Are you angry at me, Father?" she finally asked.

"What?" He looked astonished. "Of course not. What gave you that idea?"

"The look on your face," she explained. "I was afraid you might be blaming me for the fact that Phineas got away."

"Don't be silly. It's not your fault. If I'd heeded your opinion in the first place he might not have fooled me so completely."

"You shouldn't blame yourself," Tess said tenderly. "After all, you only know what you learned growing up."

That comment made her father snort derisively, much to her surprise and puzzlement.

He glanced at her. "You really don't know the whole story, do you?"

"Story of what?"

"The struggles of my youth. I didn't have a dime to my name until I married your mother. She brought her fortune into our family. All I did was invest it wisely and make it grow."

"You—you mean you weren't born rich?"

"Hardly. We were dirt poor when I was a boy. Why do you think I cared so much that you had all the best of everything? I didn't want you to struggle the way I had."

"What about your parents?"

"They died when I was in my teens, just as I always told you. What I didn't say was that I apprenticed myself to my future father-in-law at his bank in Philadelphia. That was how I learned the business and eventually met and married your mother."

"You were like Phineas! No wonder you thought he'd be perfect for me."

Gerald made a sour face. "I hadn't thought of it quite that way but I suspect you may be right."

"We shouldn't let him get away, you know." Tess had been checking side streets as they drove and although she had not seen any sign of the grocery wagon she was still hopeful. "What if we drove around a little before we headed for the park? There's always a chance we might catch a glimpse of him. I don't have a pistol with me but I don't think he was armed, either."

The astonishment on her father's face quickly became thoughtful. "I suppose there would be no particular danger as long as we stayed in the car and stuck to areas that have already burned."

"Exactly. Do you have enough fuel?"

"I poured in another gallon when I stopped at the bank. We should be fine for a while."

Tess began to grin. "In that case, let's go find that wagon and see that Phineas gets what's coming to him.

"What about your young man? We promised…"

"You promised. I didn't," Tess said, grinning. "Besides, Michael has his hands full right now. If we decide to take a little detour it won't matter to him. Not as long as we eventually end up at the park as planned."

Gerald gave her a look that was almost respectful, although Tess was sorry it had taken a series of tragedies to bring it about. She might physically resemble her late mother but that was where the similarities ended. She was smart and strong-willed, just like her father, and it was high time he gave her credit for having backbone.

Michael had helped his fellows stretch a hose line all the way from the bay. His engine and others like it had been hooked in tandem to pump the seawater up the hills but he knew the breakdown of even one engine in the line would mean failure of the entire operation.

Now he could see flames licking the sides of the

Huntington mansion. Crocker's place was next. Worse, the streets around Nob Hill were once again teeming with evacuees, folks who had not seen fit to leave earlier when their passage to safety would have been relatively easy.

"Hey! Slow down. You can't race through there," Michael yelled.

He waved his arms to no avail as wagon after wagon rolled through the intersection and crossed their canvas hoses at a pace that was nearly rapid enough to rupture them. Didn't those drivers know how fragile the heavy fabric could be when it was wet? Didn't they care that those metal-rimmed wheels were likely to cause leaks that couldn't be repaired?

Frantic, he kept trying to divert oncoming wagons. The wealthy were finally realizing that the disaster was going to reach their sanctuaries and were hurriedly attempting to rescue their expensive possessions. As far as he was concerned there was nothing on this earth as valuable as human life, yet those people continued to defy the orders of the very men who were sworn to save them.

Michael bent his back with the others who were hauling some of the heavy hose to the side of the road. Wet paving stones were slick. Hazardous. Sweat and sprays of seawater dripped from his leather helmet and stung his eyes till he could barely see.

"There goes another one," someone shouted, pointing. "Look."

Michael raised his head, blinked and wiped his

smarting eyes with a kerchief. His heart plummeted. The mansion directly next door to the Clarks' was catching fire and beginning to burn as if some malevolent force had just doused it with kerosene and touched a match to the base.

Behind him, a horn honked. He whirled, ready to block the way of whoever else intended to pass. To his horror, the automobile belonging to Gerald Clark was approaching. And Tess was still aboard.

Michael lunged toward the car and grabbed the edge of the door on the driver's side. Staring past her father, he shouted directly at Tess, almost losing control of his temper enough to curse. "What are you doing here?"

"The horses," Tess cried, pointing.

"Forget it. It's too late. You can't go up there." Michael was adamant as well as terrified for her. He grabbed her father's arm. "Go back. Can't you see what's happening?"

The car shuddered and its engine died. Gerald looked surprised. "Sorry. We saw the smoke and thought we could be of assistance. Can we do something? Anything?"

"No. If you can get this thing started again you need to turn around and leave. Otherwise you'll need to push it out of the way and walk. You can't stay here. It's too dangerous."

"All right," the older man said. "You take care of yourself—son. My daughter expects you to come out of this mess in one piece."

A brief glance at Tess confirmed how much she cared.

Michael managed a conciliatory smile for her benefit. "Don't worry. I'll find you when this is over."

Although their gazes locked he said no more. There was nothing else to say, nor was there enough time in which to say it properly. He had a duty not only to his own crew but to the other engines in the pumping line. The fire beneath each boiler had to be stoked and the buildup of steam efficiently managed in order to push every last drop of water through those long lines.

Backing away, Michael headed for his pumper as the older man climbed out of the car. At least Tess would still have an escort back to the park, even if it wasn't him. He checked the gauges on his instrument panel and saw with satisfaction that the steam pressure was holding steady. *Good.* Running this equipment was an art as much as a science and, modesty aside, he was one of the best engineers in all of San Francisco.

Another glance told him that Gerald had failed to get the car started. He and several other men were pushing it backward while Tess sat behind the wheel.

Michael gritted his teeth. He wanted to be angry with her and her father, yet he was so relieved to have seen that they were all right he couldn't manage to stir up much ire. Perhaps he'd feel differently later but right now, right here, he was simply thankful.

Tess slid from behind the wheel and climbed down as soon as she felt the rear tires contact the curb. The high color in her father's face worried her. She quickly took his hand and led him aside. "Are you all right?"

"Yes. I just need to sit and rest a bit. It's that confounded starter. I shouldn't have cranked it so much."

"I thought we had plenty of gas?"

"We should have had," Gerald replied, mopping his brow and perching on the rear bumper of the automobile. "We may have broken a fuel line during our rough travels." His eyes misted. "I should have listened to your young man and taken you straight to the park."

"Nonsense. We might have come across Phineas. It's not your fault that we didn't."

As Tess sat beside him and watched, her father looked as if he were about to weep. "It's not that. It's the money. I put it first."

"You were just thinking of your depositors."

Gerald shook his head. "No. I was thinking of the money. That was all that mattered to me. That was all that's ever mattered. Oh, I told myself I was working for the good of my family but it always came back to the same thing. The bottom line." A few tears began to streak his cheeks. "I let life pass me by."

"It's not too late, Father," Tess told him tenderly. "You still have me. We can do wonderful things together. I had thought of turning the house into a refugee center, for a short while, at least until some of these places are rebuilt and people can go home again. Or maybe it can be an orphanage for children like that poor little tyke I found in the rubble yesterday. You should see her. She's adorable."

He arched and eyebrow. "You were out on the streets?"

"Aiding the needy. With Michael." Seeking to distract

her father and keep him from drawing inappropriate conclusions, she added, "You can use your influence to help the cause of woman suffrage, too, if you wish. There are some extraordinary ladies involved in that movement."

He patted her hand. "None as extraordinary as you, I'm sure. You are truly a treasure, Tess. I wouldn't have thought we'd ever talk to each other this way and now here we are."

"I suspect we will still have our differences," she replied, smiling knowingly. "But we must always remember this day, no matter what."

Looking past him, she let her gaze wander up the hill. Her jaw dropped. The firemen had not halted the fire the way she'd assumed they would. Flames were now leaping from the roofs of the Crocker and Stanford mansions and being blown ahead like the unstoppable gale that preceded a hurricane. And her home stood next in line!

Chapter Eighteen

Michael had assumed Tess and her father had left the area because he no longer saw either of them. Smoke billowed, whirled and eddied, sometimes thick, sometimes mere wisps. Always it burned eyes and lungs. And always it filled in just when he thought he was about to see through and discern more about what was going on in the distance.

It didn't matter to him directly, of course. He didn't dare leave his post. He merely wanted to see how the nozzle men were faring and tell if his ongoing prayers for their success were being answered.

A gust of wind off the ocean caught beneath the wide, back brim of his hat and lifted it off his neck to the extent allowed by the chin strap. Michael pivoted to brace himself. The smoke ahead parted momentarily.

Far up the hill he thought he caught a glimpse of movement, of a denser gray merging with the smoke. The flash of reddish tresses and the whipping of a woman's skirt disappeared rapidly into the cloud. Could it be her? Would she be that foolish?

Taking the chance that his conclusion was right, Michael shouted, "Tess! No."

Every instinct within him was screaming that he must chase after the woman, must somehow bring her back even if she wasn't Tess. He knew he didn't dare. His specific skills were not only invaluable, they needed every hand they already had on scene and more if they hoped to make any difference in the progress of the fire. He had sworn allegiance to the fire brigade. He could not turn away. If he did, hundreds more might die as a result.

Cupping his hands around his mouth, he shouted, "Tess!" at the top of his lungs. "Tess! Come back."

The smoke darkened as if night had fallen and closed like a malevolent fist around the retreating figure, hiding even the most basic shadows as if they had never been there. As if he'd only imagined witnessing the love of his life disappear into the bowels of the inferno.

Michael moaned. His heart and soul cried out. He began to weep, silently but openly, until he was barely able to focus on the crucial gauges positioned right in front of his face.

Tess trusted her intuition to guide her through to her goal. It did. By the time she reached the estate grounds she was coughing so badly she couldn't catch her breath. Her eyes were red, swollen and burning.

Shooting pains in her ribs, caused by the intense

exertion, doubled her over. She refused to give up or turn back. Clutching her waist, she wrapped both arms around her torso and staggered on toward the stables.

The roof above the main part of the structure was already cresting with flames. Horses snorted. Whinnied in fright. Tess followed the sounds to locate her mare and the others she'd come to rescue.

She was overcome with relief to discover them all outside in a paddock instead of locked away in their stalls. *Hallelujah!* She wasn't going to have to brave fire in the barn to rescue any others.

She shut her eyes for an instant and breathed a heartfelt "Praise God."

The frantic animals were galloping in circles in the paddock, moving as a herd in hope of escape the oncoming flames. She could certainly understand their fear. Hers was palpable. And growing to the point where she was nearly beside herself.

"Easy, easy," she said, struggling to control her trembling, dampen her wheezing cough and speak to them calmly.

It was readily apparent that tone didn't matter. Those horses were not about to listen to anyone. Clearly none were calm enough for her to catch and bridle either, let alone hope to ride. She might as well have tried to throw a saddle on a wild mustang.

There was only one sensible thing to do. She unlatched the gate to offer the animals their freedom, praying that their survival instincts would be strong enough to carry them to safety.

"Here! Look!" she yelled before breaking into paroxysms of coughing and grabbing her ribs again with her free arm.

She waggled the open wooden gate back and forth to help them spot it through the haze. Her mare was the first to dash through. The others followed.

When the last horse had raced past, Tess came to her senses and took stock of the situation. The stable building was already a total loss and the house was about to join it. Fire was consuming the eucalyptus foliage above the lawn as if it was part of a line of oil-soaked torches rather than the beautiful green-and-gray shade trees she remembered.

Paroxysms of coughing shook her till she could hardly stand, let alone think of fleeing.

She fell to her knees in the dirt.

"God, help me," she muttered as smoke burned her eyes and stole the last of her sight. "What have I done?"

A hand clamped firmly on Michael's shoulder gave him a start. He wheeled. It was Chief Walters.

"It's over," the chief said. "We're shutting down and falling back. We've lost two of the pumps in the line and there are no replacements."

Rubbing his face against the sleeve of his heavy coat, Michael hoped his despondency didn't show. Truth to tell, he felt as dead as the earthquake and fire victims he'd seen lying in the streets. He'd stayed at his post and done his duty no matter what. So had the others. But it

hadn't been enough. All their pride in the fire brigades
had been for naught. San Francisco lay in ashes. And
so, he feared, did his heart.

Walters peered at him. "You look awful."

Trying to subdue a shudder, Michael pointed. "I—I
saw a woman run into the smoke a few minutes ago. It
looked like Tess Clark."

"Are you sure?"

"No," he answered honestly.

"You think it was her though, don't you?"

"Yes." Pointing to the automobile, he saw that Gerald
Clark was still resting beside it, apparently ill, while
several passersby tended to him. "She and her father
drove up together. Their car stalled. The last I saw of
her she was over there with him."

"She's the woman I saw riding with you on the rescue
wagon yesterday, isn't she?"

Michael nodded, fighting to control his emotions and
barely succeeding.

To his surprise, Walters choked back a sob. "I haven't
told anyone else this. I lost my wife in the quake."

Clapping a hand on the chief's shoulder, Michael said,
"I'm so sorry," identifying with the man's grief far more
than he liked.

"Go," Walters ordered suddenly. He gestured with
one arm and gave Michael a push with the other. "Go
find her if you can. I'll take care of shutting down your
engine."

The enormity of the other man's selflessness in the
wake of his own deep personal loss touched Michael

to the core. God might not have dispatched a guardian angel to answer his prayers but He had certainly acted when He'd sent the chief.

"Thanks," Michael shouted, beginning to race up the hill as if all his weariness had suddenly been replaced with an unending supply of strength and stamina.

He knew where he'd last seen the shadowy figure. And he knew the basic layout of the Clark estate. If it had been Tess who had disappeared into the smoke he'd find her. Or die trying.

Tess's basic instincts told her to get away from the buildings so she began to crawl, feeling her way along the ground. It was impossible to tell in which direction she was heading so she simply tried to locate enough air to sustain life.

It wasn't easy. Every time she thought she was in the clear, the wind shifted and bore down on her, as if it were a ruthless pursuer, intent on stealing her last breath and rendering her helpless.

Prayer, as she'd always practiced it, was impossible. She could barely breathe, let alone whisper a suitable appeal, so she let her thoughts cry out to God for her.

Mostly, she repeated, "Father, help me," over and over, with a few pauses for uncontrolled fits of coughing and vows of repentance. Could she expect an answer? Did she dare beg God for rescue after recklessly putting herself in such an untenable position?

Tears of sadness and physical pain bathed her eyes and wet her lashes. They dripped into the dust, sometimes landing atop the backs of her hands as she felt her way along inch by inch. At least she'd saved the horses. Or at least she thought she had. Releasing them had been the most logical option. If she'd had more time she might have tried to climb aboard her mare and let it choose a route of escape for them both. Now, it was too late.

Closing her eyes, Tess bent forward to rest her forehead on her clasped hands. Everything was becoming blurred, surreal, even the roar from the flames that were devouring the house. All she wanted to do was rest. Sleep. Let her weary mind carry her away from all this.

Suddenly, something stung the back of her neck. It felt as if a hot poker had been shoved into her hair!

Pain jolted her into alertness. Grabbing at her head to beat out the smoldering embers, she inhaled. Got a good breath. And let out a piercing scream.

Michael heard her screech and his blood chilled. It *was* Tess he'd seen walking into the smoke and she was hurt.

He braced himself, cupped his hands and answered with, "Tess! Where are you?"

No answer came. Peering in the direction he thought the noise had originated, he forged ahead.

Filling his lungs was impossible. He managed to barely gulp enough air to shout out from time to time. He stretched his arms ahead of him, feeling his way and nearly blinded by the stinging smoke.

Knowing Tess, she would have headed for the stables,

he reasoned. The first thing she'd said when she and her father had arrived was "The horses."

"Tess! Answer me."

Heavyhearted, totally spent, Michael tripped. Stumbled. One hand touched the ground. The other...

He'd found her!

Grabbing the slim shoulder where his hand had landed, he gave it a shake. "Tess! Wake up."

Unspoken prayers rose from the depths of his soul. *Please, God. Let her be all right.*

Still, she didn't stir. Didn't respond.

A flicker of fire caught his eye. There was a glowing ember in her hair!

Michael closed his hand over the fire, ignoring the singeing of his own flesh. Water. Where was the closest water?

Squinting into the drifting smoke, he spotted what he thought was the large trough he'd used when tending the team. That would more than suffice.

He had to temporarily let go of her hair in order to stand and gather her into his arms. In three long strides he'd reached the side of the wooden trough.

Without further thought he plunged Tess's whole body into the water, then briefly pushed her head under, too.

Tess popped up out of the water flailing, sputtering, dripping and gasping. Her words were hoarse and unintelligible but they were still the most wonderful sounds Michael had ever heard.

He reached for her. Pulled her partially into his arms without letting her leave the trough. "Easy. Easy. You were on fire," he said brokenly. "I had to dunk you. Thankfully, it also brought you to your senses."

She threw her arms around his neck and began to sob with an intensity beyond anything Michael had ever experienced.

His emotions were no more stable. Holding her close, he wept against her dripping hair and thanked God they'd been reunited. In moments, he realized that they were not yet safe. Far from it.

"We have to go," he said, recovering his senses enough to begin to assess the situation. "Can you tell which way the street lies?"

Tess shook her head. "No. I got terribly turned around. Then I fell and..." Clinging tighter, she was wracked with renewed sobs and coughing.

"Pull yourself together," Michael ordered. "Think. After you let the horses loose, which way did they run?"

"I—I—I don't know."

"Yes, you do. You're sitting in their watering trough. Use that to get your bearings."

Straightening, she peered into the thick air. "I can't see a thing."

"Neither could those horses but I'd trust their judgment over mine any day." He got to his feet and helped her climb out of the water. Her clothing and hair were soaked and dripping, which was exactly the way he wanted her to be. "Now, which way?"

Tess sagged against him. He knew she was nearly

spent but he needed her advice if they hoped to find sanctuary.

He tightened his grip around her shoulder and insisted, "Tess. Come on. You can do this. Which way did they go?"

Slowly lifting her arm as if it weighed tons, she pointed. "That way."

Michael stopped himself from asking if she was certain. At this juncture there was no use delaying. If she was mistaken and they fled into a worse conflagration instead of a safe zone, they would meet death together.

His jaw clenched. No. That would not happen. They would get through, somehow. God had brought them this far. He would not abandon them now.

Tess's head was swimming. She still wasn't sure whether Michael's presence was a figment of her imagination or if he was truly there. She even doubted the chill of her wet clothing at first. The last thing she recalled clearly was falling to her knees and folding her hands in preparation for meeting her Maker.

The rest of the time was a blur. Her legs felt as limp as the ribbons that bound her mother's journal. If this was all imaginary, then perhaps she would soon see Mama face-to-face in heaven.

At her side, she sensed the strength that was Michael. Blinking, she looked up and saw the beard stubble on his chin. This could *not* be a dream. It was far too real. There was fire and smoke all around them. She could

barely see him, let alone discern their path. Where were
they going?

Coughing, she managed to say his name, "Michael?"

"I've got you. We'll make it," he replied.

"I'm so sorry."

His hold tightened. "Let's get out of this mess first.
We can talk about other things later."

"I love you," Tess said before breaking into more
paroxysms of coughing.

"Yeah," he answered gruffly. "I know. And I love you,
too, even if you are crazy brave."

That was enough to satisfy Tess. If this was a dream it
was turning out exactly the way she'd always envisioned.
And if it was real, as she hoped, she had just heard the
man she planned to spend the rest of her life with say
he returned her love.

"Thank You, Jesus," she whispered, feeling a sur-
prising surge of energy and a renewed lightness of her
steps.

She gazed lovingly up at her gallant fireman. "You'll
get us out of this. I know you will."

"I'm sorry about your house."

"It was just a building," Tess said. Eyes inflamed and
streaming tears in reaction to the constant irritation, she
peered ahead. "Look! I think the smoke is clearing."

Although he didn't immediately say he agreed, he
did pick up their pace. When she had trouble moving
fast enough to keep up with him, he swung her into his
arms and carried her.

Tess wrapped her arm around his neck and hung

on tightly, placing her cheek against his shoulder as he began to trot. A sound rumbled deep in Michael's chest and at first she thought he might be crying.

Then, as they broke into the open and were able to see that they were truly safe, she realized he was laughing.

Bearing his wondrous burden into the center of the street where they'd be clear of any threat from either fire or collapsing structures, Michael set Tess on her feet and doubled over, hands on his knees, trying to catch his breath.

"Where are we?"

He rose and scanned their surroundings. "Columbia Street, I think." Laughter continued to bubble up in spite of his breathlessness. "I can't believe it. We made it!"

"Only because of you."

When she grasped his hand he realized he hadn't escaped unscathed. Although he tried not to show pain, she noticed his flinch and turned his palm up.

"What happened? When were you burned?"

He knew all too well and, given their shared elation, he figured this was a good time to tell her. "I think I did it putting out the fire in the back of your hair."

Tess looked so astonished he had to assume she didn't remember.

"That was the main reason I dunked you in the horse trough. You do recall that, don't you?"

"Oh, yes." She made a face as she glanced at her sopping skirt and jacket. "I thought you were trying to drown me."

"Never," Michael said, grinning so widely his cheeks ached. "I might consider spanking you if you tried anything that reckless again, though."

She stepped back, hands fisted on her hips. "You wouldn't dare!"

Chuckling, smiling and shaking his head, he said, "You're right. I wouldn't. But not because I'm afraid of you, Miss Clark. I'd never lay a hand on you because I love you. I saw what that kind of rough treatment did to my mother and I want you to always trust me. I'd never harm you."

Spreading his arms, he wordlessly invited her back into his embrace. As soon as she was snuggled against him he broke the news that he'd have to be getting back to duty.

Tess's hug tightened. "Must you?"

"Yes. Chief Walters released me to go after you but I owe him as much more work as I'm capable of. You have to understand that."

"Of course," Tess said, although she didn't sound very convinced.

"We can cut around to Powell and probably get through there, now that that part of the fire has burned out. When you rejoin your father and head for the park, remember that and try to travel where it's already burned. Just stay away from those idiots with the dynamite."

"Blowing up things is not working very well, is it?"

Michael sighed, disgusted and discouraged. "It might have, in the right hands. Most of the men who were given the job of placing the charges had no experience. I suspect they did more harm than good."

As he drew her to his side and began to escort her toward their destination he realized how fatigued he was. Not only had he spent several a night without sleeping, he'd worked at top capacity since morning.

Smiling to himself, he glanced down at the precious woman beside him. He had vowed to give his life to save her if necessary and he would have kept that promise if it had come to that.

Now, however, his heart was overflowing with gratitude for the privilege of remaining with her. Their chances of mutual survival had been slim to none. Yet here they were. Together.

He bent to place a kiss atop her head, not minding the dampness of her hair or the perfume of smoke.

"I hope I didn't lose too much when it burned," Tess said, patting the back of her neck to investigate. "I have a notion you like my hair."

"I love *everything* about you and I always will, with or without your beautiful hair," he said honestly.

She giggled. "Does that include my stubborn streak?"

"Let's just say I'm working on accepting that." His laughter melded with hers. "I suspect it may take me a while longer, especially if you keep exercising it the way you did today."

"I really am sorry I did such a stupid thing."

"I know you are. Hopefully you're a lot smarter now."

"I was smart enough to fall in love with you in spite

of my father." She laughed softly, then went on. "You aren't going to believe the secrets I learned about him today. He and I are a lot more alike than I'd thought."

"As long as he accepts me as I am and doesn't try to put me to work in his bank, I'll be satisfied," Michael said.

"Oh, what a marvelous idea!"

He stiffened. His eyes widened and he stared at her. Then she followed her statement with another giggle and eased his mind. "Don't scare me like that. I thought you were serious."

"Never," Tess told him. "I love you just as you are. And I absolutely *adore* firemen."

Chapter Nineteen

Tess was astounded at the visible change of the whole area by the time she and Michael arrived at the spot where she'd left her father. The street was as wet as it would have been after a rain. Gangs of firemen had been uncoupling the hoses, breaking them into shorter lengths and rolling them up. Most of the steam pumpers had already left.

Michael took her hand, led her over to Chief Walters, and proudly announced, "I found her!"

When Tess saw the pathos in the other man's expression she was more than touched.

He and Michael had been sharing an exuberant handshake. As soon as they stopped, she also offered her hand. The chief took it. Like her, he was smiling through unshed tears.

"Thank you," Tess said. "Thank you for letting Michael come after me."

"Rules are made to be broken, especially in times like these," Walters replied. He eyed her from head to toe. "Are you all right?"

"I will be." Another coughing fit made her pause.

"It can take a long time to get over breathing in that much smoke," he cautioned. "Be sure you take it real easy for a while."

"I will." Thinking of Michael having to go back to work and fight fire when he'd been exposed to as much flying soot and ash as she had, she was crestfallen. Part of that harm to his lungs was her fault. So was the burn on his hand.

She saw both men glance toward the idle automobile so she asked, "Is my father still around?"

"No," Walters said. "He was acting ill so I sent him down the hill on one of the other engines."

"Ill? Oh, dear!"

"Don't worry, miss. I doubt there was anything wrong with him that one look at you won't cure. He was so beside himself after he lost sight of you, he started raving and shouting but not making a bit of sense. He refused to listen to reason. I had to have some men force him aboard the pumper and hold him there to get him to leave."

She felt Michael's arm tighten around her shoulders, offering the same moral support on which she had grown so reliant.

"How about letting me drive Tess?" he asked. "At least as far as my next assignment?"

To her relief and joy, the chief nodded immediately. "That's what I figured to do." He began to smile. "I didn't see much point in your risking your life to get her this far and then making her walk all the way to the park."

"Is that where you sent Papa?" she asked.

"Yes. Nurses and doctors who had to evacuate from the emergency center in the basement of city hall are set up in Golden Gate Park." He nodded at Michael. "Our hose wagons will handle the rest of this mess. Drive the young lady as far as the park, then rendezvous at the ferry terminal again for new orders."

Michael saluted. "Yes, sir."

In parting, Tess once again reached for the chief's hand. "God bless you," she said. To her amazement he nodded brusquely, then turned on his heel and strode away.

When she looked up at Michael there was shared sorrow on his face. He bent to whisper, "Chief Walters's wife was killed in the earthquake."

"Oh, no." Her hand went to her throat, her heart breaking for the poor man's loss. "No wonder he was so willing to let you come after me."

"Yeah. I'd thought of that, too."

Michael checked the harness on his team while she waited, then helped her climb onto the driver's seat before joining her.

She slipped her hand through the crook of his elbow, marveling at how natural that action had become. It seemed as if she and Michael were already one in the eyes of God, the way they truly would be after they were married.

She sighed, basking in his nearness and drinking in the blessings of their time together as though it might yet be limited. Her heart was torn between peace and trepidation, happiness and grief, aspirations of a bright future and lingering dread.

Tightening her hold, she smiled at him. He mirrored the gesture. They were both still coughing at times but the hacking hoarseness seemed to be lessening. It hurt her to breathe deeply and her throat felt raw so she assumed Michael was also experiencing those detrimental aftereffects.

And he was headed back to face even more.

"I want you to promise me something," he said, concentrating primarily on driving the team instead of watching Tess. He was afraid if he said what was on his mind and saw her start to cry he might not be able to keep his own emotions in check. The last thing he wanted to do was let her see him weep. Especially since he couldn't blame his tears on the effects of the smoke the way he had before.

"Of course. Anything." She laughed lightly, nervously. "Well, almost anything."

"Good girl."

"I may be good, but I'm no longer a girl," Tess argued genially. "I guess you noticed that."

"Oh, yes." Chancing a quick smile at her, he was amazed by how lovely she was, even in such a bedraggled condition. He chuckled. "You don't look quite up to snuff right now but I have an excellent memory. I remember you at your best."

"I am a sight, aren't I?" Making a silly face at him, she started rubbing at the dirt streaking her soggy skirt.

"It's all your fault. This used to be a lovely afternoon outfit."

"That's the problem, then," he joked back. "There was nothing *lovely* about this afternoon. You wore the wrong dress to the party."

"I must have. It's certainly ruined." Shaking her head slowly, pensively, she stopped trying to spruce up her clothing. "Given what I went through while wearing it, I'm glad it can't be salvaged. I'd certainly not want to put it on again. Too many bad memories."

That was the perfect opening for Michael to speak. No matter how hard it was to voice these thoughts, he knew it must be done. Soon.

"Speaking of memories," he said, fighting to keep his tone even and his voice strong, "I want you to promise me that if anything should happen to me, today or any day, you'll go on with your life and keep trusting the Lord."

"Don't be silly. Nothing's going to happen to you."

"Just the same, I want your promise."

"Oh, Michael. How can you ask that of me? I don't even want to think about what my life might be like without you."

He held firm. "Promise, Tess. Say it. I need to hear it from you."

"It's that important to you?"

"Yes. It's that important."

Waiting, he could feel her trembling, even through the sleeve of his heavy coat. She had a tender heart, a woman's heart, despite all her bravado and the outlandish emancipation ideas she'd adopted.

"All right," she finally said. "I promise that if anything happens to you to keep us from getting married I will go on with my life."

He would have felt a lot better about her vow if she had not followed it with, "But if you think you're going to weasel out of marrying me, Michael Mahoney, you'd better think again."

It would have pleased Tess to have arrived at the family camp aboard the fire engine and been able to show it off to the children, at least. Unfortunately, Michael stopped outside the park perimeter.

"You'll need to walk from here," he said. "Can you manage?"

"Yes." Every fiber of her being kept insisting that she could not possibly leave him, yet she knew she must. When he kept hold of the reins instead of climbing down to assist her, she was puzzled.

Michael gave her his trademark Irish grin and wound the three pair of lines around the brake lever before opening his arms. "Come here, darlin'. Kiss your future husband goodbye."

"That's more like it," Tess said, throwing herself into his embrace. "You had me a little worried."

"Never worry about my love for you, no matter what," he whispered against her cheek, his breath tickling her ear. "I'll love you forever."

That was almost more than Tess's fragile frame of

mind could bear. He sounded as though he was bidding her a final farewell because he didn't expect to return. The mere thought of that happening made her heart clench.

Leaning away just far enough to cup his beard-roughened cheeks in her hands, she held his face still and gazed into his eyes, willing him to share her belief. "You are coming back to me, do you hear? I am not going to take no for an answer. You know how stubborn I am, right? Well, this is how it's going to be."

To her relief, he didn't look angry. On the contrary, his smile spread. "Are you finished?"

"Yes," Tess said, "providing you've been listening to me."

"I've been listening."

"Then don't even think of arguing."

"Yes, ma'am."

She knew he was teasing her by making fun of her seriousness but she didn't care. This was the note on which she wanted them to part—happy, smiling and sharing a kiss that would carry them both through to the end of this crisis.

Pulling him closer, her hands still holding his cheeks, she placed her lips on his and felt his tender response. She knew they both looked a fright and that neither cared one iota. All that mattered was this expression of love and the promise of a bright future.

Tess held on even after Michael started to ease her away. Her eyes were closed, her heart open.

"We're drawing a crowd, darlin'," Michael drawled.

"I think I'd best let you jump down and be on my way. Don't want the good citizens of San Francisco complaining about misuse of fire department equipment."

Her eyes popped open. He was right! "Oh, my! We do have an audience, don't we?"

"Afraid so." Taking her hand, he helped her step past his booted feet to the edge of the platform, then carefully lowered her over the side of the pumper till she gained her footing.

That was when the applause and cheering began. Tess's cheeks flamed. Unsure of what to do, she simply curtsied as if answering a curtain call from the stage of the opera.

Atop the engine Michael removed his hat and took his own bow, much to the added delight of passersby, before calling to the team and starting to pull slowly away.

Stepping back, Tess waved gaily after him, hoping he hadn't spied her misty eyes. She was not going to cry. Especially not in front of him. He *would* come back to her.

He must. Because if he didn't there was no way she'd be able to keep her promise and go on with her life. Whether he realized it or not, Michael Mahoney *was* her life.

The route Tess followed to wend her way through the masses of tents was, by necessity, meandering. The actual distance from the gate to their camp, however, was short. Tess was more than glad of that since her legs ached from running almost as much as her ribs and chest did from coughing.

She would have liked to make herself more presentable before returning to friends and family but if what the chief had said was true, poor Papa wouldn't care how dreadful she looked.

Ducking around a clothesline that some optimistic soul had hung between two trees to dry laundry, she burst into the clearing with a light heart and heavy limbs. Weariness threatened to overcome her at any moment.

Annie was the first to give an ecstatic shriek and alert everyone. In seconds Tess was surrounded by the other women and the two older children, all hugging her, babbling and shouting questions that were so overlapped none were clear.

"Wait. Please," Tess said, holding up her hands. "I'll tell you everything soon." She scanned the campsite. "But first I need to see Papa. Is he here?"

"Sleeping," Mary said. "Rose got a powder from one of the nurses and we put it in his coffee. He's finally resting. He was in a sorry state. Near hysterical, he was. Such a pity."

"I know. I heard," Tess replied. "They told me it was all because of me. I must see him."

Edging past the children and giving them each a pat on the head, she was relieved that neither they nor the adults insisted on following her.

Shadows inside the shelter were made deeper by the layer of soot that had accumulated on the outside. She paused. The still form of Gerald Clark lay on a pallet in the midst of what few household goods they had managed to gather.

Tess's hand went to her throat. Her jaw dropped open. She stared and whispered prayerfully, "Thank You, Jesus."

It made sense to want to weep for joy when she and her father were finally reunited. What she had not expected was to be so shocked by his appearance. Papa had always seemed invincible. Strong. Competent. Now, lying there with his back to her he looked frail, his gray hair mussed and his clothing rumpled and grimy.

She approached him slowly, quietly, giving thanks that his breathing was even and his rest apparently untroubled.

Pausing behind him and looking down, she spied a second surprise. There, cradled in the sanctuary provided by the curve of her father's sleeping form, lay the darling orphan child she had rescued. The baby's fingers were curled around Papa's hand and she, too, was fast asleep.

Unembarrassed and astonished, Tess just stood there and gazed at the unexpected sight. After everything that had happened to them and to the whole city she knew she was being given a special gift. Seeing Papa—her papa—showing tenderness to a child that wasn't even his own was more than unforeseen. It was unbelievable.

Rare blessings like this one might be occurring all over the city, she realized. Even terrible catastrophes could result in changes for the good.

The babe stirred. Tess saw her father gently stroke its curly, blond hair and heard him whisper, "Hush."

Rather than startle him by announcing her presence and perhaps frighten the little child as well, Tess quietly fell to her knees beside the pallet, rested her hand on his shirtsleeve and merely said, "Papa."

Gerald sat bolt upright, jaw gaping, and clamped her in an embrace that was so tight it hurt. "Tess! I thought…"

"I know," she said, patting his back. "I got lost in the smoke. I would probably have died if Michael hadn't come after me."

"I didn't see where you went," Gerald managed to say before breaking down. "I looked away for a minute and when I turned around you were just *gone*."

"Michael saw me, praise the Lord, and his chief let him follow. I went up the hill to save the horses."

"*Horses?* You risked your life for animals?"

"I know it was foolish," she admitted. "But all I could think about was doing something—anything. It seemed as if everybody was failing no matter how hard they fought." She eased herself away from him to watch his face when she said, "The fire took the house. Everything is gone. Ashes."

Gerald was adamant. "Who cares? It's just a house. And the funds Phineas took aren't important either. I never should have driven you up there where you could get hurt."

"It's okay," Tess said soothingly. "I'm here now. There's lots of help coming in on the ferries and the army has been mobilized, too. This terrible peril can't last forever."

Even as she said the words, Tess wondered if she was right. Logic said she was. The experiences of the past couple of days, however, demonstrated that this trial would not end quickly or without even more loss of life.

Picturing Michael, she once again said a silent prayer for his deliverance. She wanted to trust God. Wanted to rest in the promises of scripture. Really, she did.

Then in a flash she remembered the collapse of building after building, the cries of the injured, the relentless march of the inferno, and her assurance fled like the smoke that was covering the city and its shores.

Gerald Clark lifted the dozing babe and started to hand her to Tess before he took note of her sooty clothing.

He stopped abruptly and smiled. "Look at you. I suspect I'd better take charge of this little one for a while longer." Struggling stiffly to his feet, he led the way out of the shelter. "I want you to tell me everything, even the bad parts, and I'm sure the others would like to hear all about your adventures, too. Shall we go sit with them?"

"Of course." A wide grin lit her face, too. "I am *very* glad to see you—to see everyone, Papa." Amused, she eyed the babe he was cradling. "I must admit, you are not the same man I thought you were."

"No one is the same after this," her father said, joining the others and handing the babe to Rose. "Now, sit down and tell us your story."

Just then the ground shook again and all over the park people froze in midmotion, waiting and hoping the tremors would stop rather than worsen.

How many earthquakes did this make since the big one? Tess wondered. She doubted anyone was still trying to keep track of the number of aftershocks. Truth to tell, she was beyond caring. There was no sensible course but to face one day at a time.

There was one thing she did intend to count, however. The hours and days until she and Michael Mahoney were together again.

Chapter Twenty

The next few days passed so quickly Tess was amazed. By Saturday morning, most of the fires had burned themselves out and those that were still smoldering were doused by most welcome showers that also helped clear the air.

Occasional rain complicated life in the park little. Most of the campers stayed warm and dry because the army had provided thousands of tents as well as the manpower to help erect them. Trainloads of other necessities had started arriving from as far away as New York to the east and Oregon and Washington to the north. Boats also continued to ferry supplies and workers over via ports in Oakland.

Tess had taken Rachel and David to the rail depot with her several times, ostensibly to help her tote an allotment of bread and milk. The little boy hadn't been much actual help but she knew he needed to feel useful to fend off melancholy.

She was the same way. Each hour that passed she

grew more anxious to see Michael again, and if she dared let herself dwell on her emotions she got worse. Thankfully Annie had been able to dress her hair in a way that hid the burned-off place and she'd found a nice black skirt and white blouse to wear after she'd scrubbed herself clean. The only other thing she yearned to show Michael was how well she'd recovered.

Thanks to their newly erected tent, Rose and Mary had arranged comfortable quarters for everyone, even setting aside a special private corner for her father while the women and children bunked together. The sight of the usually stuffy banker snoring peacefully atop a quilt spread on the ground was truly a wonder to behold.

Tess supposed, given the fact that Papa was the senior member of their group and was still recovering from all the smoke he'd breathed, he did deserve individual consideration. It seemed to her that the older women were fussing over him too much though. Rose in particular.

Keeping as busy as possible, Tess had sent David to one of the lakes that lay inside the park boundaries to fetch a bucket of wash water. By the time he staggered back to their tent he'd spilled most of it. Nevertheless, she greeted his efforts with praise.

"Thank you so much," she said, relieving him of the pail. "Why don't you go ask Mrs. Dugan for a cookie?"

Shaking his head and staring at the ground, he scuffed his toes through the trampled grass.

"Why not? You've earned a reward." Reaching out,

she put one finger beneath his chin and tilted up his face. There were tears in his eyes. "What's wrong?"

"I want my mama to bake me cookies."

"Oh, honey." Crouching and pulling him closer, she rubbed his bony back through the fabric of his shirt to soothe him while she tried to think of a suitable distraction.

"Tell you what," Tess said brightly, keeping one arm around his shoulders and combing his thick hair off his forehead with the fingers of her other hand. "Why don't you and I both go back for more water? Then we can carry twice as much."

David sniffled and wiped his nose on his sleeve. "Okay."

Comforting words failed her so she merely acted the part of the boy's boon companion. His sister, Rachel, being older, understood that their parents were missing and probably deceased. But poor little David was still hoping, still looking up expectantly at every passing lady as if one of them might turn out to be his mother.

If Tess had known what the woman looked like she would gladly have continued to search the thousand-plus acres of the park long after the children had grown too weary to go on. All Rachel thought she remembered was that her mother had been wearing a light blue dress right before the earthquake had leveled their home. Considering the number of refugees packed into the sea of tents and still wandering the streets, finding one particular woman in a blue dress was like looking for a needle in a haystack. And that was assuming the woman was still wearing the same clothing.

Message boards had sprung up in the most unlikely places. Unfortunately, recent downpours had destroyed many of the scrawled messages soon after they'd been posted and there was a shortage of paper and pencil with which to communicate further.

Walking beside her, David tentatively put his small hand in Tess's. She was touched. He might not understand how deeply she grieved for him but he was apparently sensing her concern, her empathy.

Only seconds had stood between her and death. She knew that now. If Michael had not come after her, she would have died just as so many others had. Although she was grateful for life, she also felt guilty for having survived when so many other worthy souls had been lost.

Beside her, the boy tensed and tugged on her hand.

"What is it, honey?"

He pointed down a row of tents. "Is that my mama?"

Tess bent next to him to follow his line of sight so she'd be sure she was looking in the right place. "I don't know. Do you think it may be?"

Shoulders slumping with dejection, he finally shook his head and said, "No. That lady's too old. My mama's prettier, too."

Tess was about to ask if he wanted to go take a closer look just in case, when she spotted something she had certainly not expected. The bowler, the cane, the prim way of almost strutting when he walked. It was him. There was no mistake. It was Phineas Edgerton!

Eyes wide, she cast around for landmarks, finding few. She and David were walking along the main concourse but where exactly were they? If she left there to go back to get help she might never be able to locate this place again. Not only that, Phineas might decide to flee while she was gone.

Crouching, she took the boy by the shoulders, held him still to look him in the eyes and spoke seriously. "I have a very special job for you, David. Do you think you can do it?"

"Uh-huh."

"Okay. Give me your bucket to hold. I want you to run back to our tent and fetch my papa as fast as you can. You know who I mean?"

Because the child appeared apprehensive, Tess added, "He's really a nice man but he's been kind of sick so he sometimes sounds cross. He'll be very happy when you tell him what I want."

She paused, making sure the child was still paying close attention, then continued, "Tell him I found the man who stole the money. And tell him to bring a gun with him when he comes to meet me. I'm going to wait right here so we don't get confused and look in the wrong place. Do you understand all that?"

"Uh-huh."

"Okay. Go. Hurry. Run."

Watching the spry little boy race back the way they'd come, Tess was torn. She wanted to stomp up to Phineas, slap his smug face and tell him exactly what she thought of him. A few days ago she might have done exactly that, even though she'd known better. Now, however, she was going to force herself to wait. Running headlong into danger had almost gotten her killed. She owed it to Michael—and to herself—to listen to her brain, not her heart, for a change.

Mopping up after a blaze was one of the hardest parts of firefighting. It was not only tedious, it was boring. There was no excitement, just smoldering ashes, the stench of burned wood and the flotsam that was all that remained of people's hopes and dreams.

Michael hadn't seen Tess or his mother or any of the others in longer than he liked. Soon that separation would be over. He wasn't particularly keen on facing Tess's father again until he'd had a chance to speak privately with her but he wanted to see her so badly he'd have faced a cage full of hungry lions to do so.

That thought made him smile. Gerald Clark did roar like a lion at times, although there was a good possibility that the banker was little more than a pussycat once he dropped all the bluster. Time would tell.

Picturing Tess, his lovely Tess, brought a grin to Michael's face. He needed sleep. And a shave. And above all a bath. He knew he should at least try to make himself more presentable before he called on her, even in the park. By now, she would have had plenty of chances to spruce up and he felt he needed to do the same in order to show his respect.

The army had set up a facility in which all the men could refresh themselves, both citizen volunteers and those who had been laboring in an official capacity like him. If he hadn't been near the Presidio when he was finally released from duty he might have thrown good manners aside and hurried to the park just as he was. However, given the ideal circumstances, he decided to tarry just long enough to bathe, shave and try to find a decent, clean change of clothes.

Then he would answer the calling of his heart and rejoin Tess. He didn't care how weary he was or how much his whole being insisted he must have rest. There would be no sleep for him until he had found Tess. Until he knew she was all right and showed her that he was fine, too.

Michael began to smile again as he visualized their glad reunion. If she missed him half as much as he missed her, there was going to be a lot more opportunity for the groups of survivors to ogle them and cheer.

Tess was pacing, off to one side of the walkway, while keeping an eagle eye on the last place she'd seen Phineas. If it looked as if he was going to escape before Papa got there she'd have to do something. But what? She didn't dare accost the weasel of a man, regardless of how appealing that move sounded. She was not only unarmed, she'd promised David that she'd wait right there for him.

Standing on tiptoe and straining to peer into the

distance, she kept watching for some sign that her father was on his way. There was plenty of activity all around her, in and out of the park, but no sign of Papa.

Tess turned back. She could see Phineas doing something. Was he moving away or merely gesturing to someone? It was impossible to tell anything from this great a distance.

"Heavenly Father, help," she prayed in a whisper. Surely, God had not brought her onto this particular path at this exact moment to show her the evil person she sought, then snatch him away again?

She fisted her hands, barely noticing the slight soreness left on her palms after having felt her way along the ground during the fire at the estate.

Her heart leaped at the vivid memory. She'd been ready to give up. Resigned to her fate. And then Michael had arrived and had saved her.

Michael. That was who she needed this time, too, she reasoned. He could make short work of Phineas and see that he didn't get away with anything else. Reflecting on the past, Tess wished she'd let the two men duke it out when they'd had their confrontation in front of the pavilion. Then perhaps Phineas wouldn't have taken his ire out on her father.

That notion brought her up short. Was *that* what this was all about? Instead of being a simple robbery, could Edgerton's actions have been more of a prideful vendetta against her family? It was possible, even probable, given the way her father had tried to engineer their courtship and she had refused to even consider it.

Staring into the distance, deep in reminiscences, Tess almost missed seeing Phineas mount a horse and prepare to depart.

The instant she came to her senses and realized what she was seeing, her heart began to pound. The option of easily confronting him had just been removed. Neither she nor Papa would be able to catch a running horse and they had none of their own to ride in pursuit. Not yet. He had sent word for his cohorts to keep an eye out for the horses she'd released, especially her mare, but so far there had been no word on their whereabouts.

Freezing in place, feeling as if her feet were rooted to the ground more solidly than the tree under which she stood, Tess saw a change in the rider's position. Not only was he reining his mount around, he looked as if he was about to charge in her direction!

"Papa, where are you?" she moaned, quickly checking the course to their camp. She didn't see any sign of either her father or the boy.

What she did see, however, was Phineas cantering toward her, riding casually as if he hadn't a care in the world.

The closer he drew, the angrier she became. He was going to pass right by her as though she didn't even exist.

Tess steeled herself. No, he wasn't. Fate had brought him into her sphere of influence and she intended to act.

Raising her arms and waving them with the express intention of frightening his horse, she stepped into his path and managed to scream, "Stop, thief!" once before breaking into the uncontrollable, racking cough that still plagued her.

Chapter Twenty-One

Striding purposefully into Golden Gate Park, his energy amazingly restored by a bath and the thought of seeing Tess again, Michael made straight for the camping area she had been occupying. Everything looked different since the addition of real tents and he prayed that she and the others hadn't decided to move to another location. If that were the case, there was no telling how long it might take to find them.

He rounded a corner. Something lightweight and short crashed into his knee, nearly knocking him over. He made a grab and came up with a handful of shirt and collar. Inside the shirt was a wriggling, dark-haired little boy.

When Michael recognized him as the one he and Tess had rescued, he smiled. "Hello, there. Take it easy, okay? Don't be runnin' around like that."

The child twisted to get away. "Let me go."

"I will, I will. Settle down. I'm not going to hurt you. Your name is David, right?"

Still the boy thrashed, adding swift though thankfully wildly inaccurate kicks to his efforts. "Let go!"

"All right, all right." Shaking his head, Michael loosened his grip and watched the frantic child speed straight for a large tent that now occupied the space where Tess and Annie had first camped.

As far as Michael was concerned, bumping into that particular boy had been the answer to his prayers. If this was where the child was staying, Tess was probably there, too.

Michael squared his shoulders, took a shaky breath and prepared himself for the blessed reunion he had feared they might never share. He was home. Moments away from seeing the only woman he had ever loved and taking her in his arms.

He got within several yards of the front flap of the tent before the boy burst out, followed by a wild-eyed version of G. B. Clark. The man was wielding one of the pistols Tess had liberated from the estate prior to its destruction by fire. The pistol's mate was stuck through Michael's belt.

Making a grab at Clark as he passed, Michael was astonished to see the barrel of the gun swing around and point right at his midsection.

He threw his hands into the air and stepped back. "Whoa! Don't shoot. It's me. What's going on?"

The look of frenzy in the older man's eyes didn't lessen but he did lower the weapon to his side. He was already gasping for air and hardly able to speak clearly enough to make himself understood.

"Run," he ordered, shoving the pistol's grip into Michael's hand. "Follow the boy."

"Why?"

All the older man had to say in addition was "Tess," for Michael to spring into action. He didn't care what the problem was. If it involved Tess, which was certainly the way things looked, nothing in the world was going to keep him from catching that fleet-footed child.

Tess wasn't convinced that Phineas's galloping horse would be able to stop before it crashed into her. Calling upon her knowledge of horses, she held her ground in the center of the path, praying she was right about equine instincts and capabilities. Not every horse had a lot of horse sense, which had always made her question how that odd saying had gained such common usage.

Standing firm, she braced herself, feet apart, preparing to dodge in the opposite direction of whatever course the horse ultimately chose.

Wild-eyed and snorting, it not only spied and heeded her, it did its best to react in a sensible, timely manner by putting on the brakes. If Tess had been asked how she would have preferred to see this encounter end, especially in view of her untenable position, she knew she could not have imagined a more perfect result.

Then, it got even better. Instead of merely sliding to a halt by squatting on its haunches and bracing itself, the horse began rearing on its hind legs and giving voice to its fears with a piercing whinny.

"Whoa!" Phineas shouted.

Tess echoed his cry. Still holding her arms aloft, she jumped up and down and yelled, "Whoa. Whoa. Easy, boy."

There must have been something soothing about her voice or perhaps her self-assurance, she concluded, because the horse gave one last leap, then stopped, snorted and came to her with its head lowered as if reporting for duty to a new master.

The poor thing was quivering. So was she. Taking hold of its bridle, she ducked, fully expecting Phineas to try to apply his quirt and begin whipping either the horse or her. Or both.

That didn't happen. Nothing else did. Puzzled, she glanced at the saddle. It was empty. Looking behind, she saw the odious little man lying flat on his back in one of the mud puddles that had been left after the rain.

He was moving his arms and legs and cursing, so he probably wasn't hurt too badly, Tess decided, stifling a grin. She refused to agree when her naughty side urged her to be glad he'd fallen. Instead, she settled for rejoicing over the fact that he had not escaped for a second time.

Suddenly, strong arms grabbed her from behind. Had Phineas had cohorts? Were they going to harm her because she'd thwarted his flight?

Tess released her hold on the horse's bridle and screeched, "No!" at the top of her voice, causing the animal to rear again and almost hit her with its flying front hooves when it came back down.

She was quickly swung out of imminent danger.

Twisting and writhing, she struggled to break free. Those arms held her like iron bands, pinning her own upper arms to her side so she couldn't fight back and lifting her feet off the ground to deprive her of traction.

She kicked. Screamed. Gasped to draw breath against the tightness of the hold. Fought until she was so spent she wondered if she might swoon.

Then, out of the blue, she thought she heard her captor say, "Tess," and froze to listen.

Again it came, echoing in her ears and settling in her heart. "Tess."

She went limp, barely able to stand let alone support herself. Cradling her gently, Michael turned her to face him and accept his embrace.

Speechless, she clung to him. Nothing else mattered. Nothing else registered in her consciousness. All she could do was wrap her arms around his waist and hug him with every ounce of love and gladness she possessed.

He began kissing her hair, the top of her head, then bent to brush his lips across her cheek before pulling her close again. Time stopped. The only thing Tess could hear was the beating of their hearts in rapid unison.

She would gladly have stood there basking in Michael's presence for the rest of her life.

Then her father's voice and the sound of his deep cough stirred her senses and she remembered what she had been doing before Michael had arrived.

Keeping her arms around his waist she nevertheless

looked over at the older man. He was red-faced and obviously laboring to breathe.

"I did it! I found him, Papa." She pointed to where the thief had landed. "Look. I stopped Phineas."

To her chagrin, Michael eased his hold. When she lifted her glance to him she saw anger where she had expected to find undying love. His mouth was firm. His eyes had narrowed. And there was a definite frown on his face that had not been there before.

"I didn't go looking for trouble, if that's what you're thinking," Tess explained. "David and I were on our way to fetch wash water and I happened to spot Phineas down one of the side roads."

Although Michael was definitely listening, it was evident he had not yet put aside his ire.

"What would you have had me do?" Tess asked, stepping back and fisting her hands on her hips. "I sent David to fetch Papa and a pistol. I waited out of sight." She rolled her eyes. "I didn't want to just stand there but I did. For you."

"For me?" One dark eyebrow twitched.

"Yes, for you. I didn't want you—or anyone—to have to come to my rescue again because I'd acted stupidly, so I was behaving myself."

"That'll be the day," Michael said.

Studying his expression, Tess was positive she'd seen one corner of his mouth lift slightly. His forehead was beginning to smooth out, too. And happily, there was more twinkle and less anger reflected in his eyes.

She took the chance that he was softening and let

herself smile slightly as she said, "I suppose you will insist that you have just saved me again, in spite of my own considerable valor in this instance."

"I might."

Her smile grew at the sight of his lopsided effort to mirror her expression. "Okay. Have it your way. If you insist on keeping track, we'll count this as your second heroic rescue." Continuing to tease in the hopes it would lift his spirits even more, she made an exaggerated curtsy. "I thank you, kind sir."

"You're welcome." Michael offered the pistol back to Gerald after using its barrel to gesture toward Phineas. "One of us needs to see to *that*."

Tess looked, too. The wiry banker was starting to crawl out of the mud and although he wasn't moving very fast, he nonetheless would bear close watching.

"Don't shoot him, Papa," she warned, seeing the fervor in Gerald's eyes as he accepted the gun. "I didn't see any sign of the wagon he was driving so we don't know where all the money went." She laughed lightly. "And don't tell me it doesn't matter. We need to find it. If not for you, at least for the sake of the depositors."

"You're right," her father said. Although he was shaking his head at her, Tess could tell he was pleased. Perhaps all these challenging events had helped him see that she was a capable person rather than a helpless woman.

Now, if she could just convince Michael of the same thing, she figured she'd be in good shape.

"Am I forgiven yet?" Tess asked him.

"I'm thinking about it."

"Well, don't dally too long," she quipped, glancing at Phineas as her father poked him into action with the gun barrel at his back. "I do have one other suitor, you know."

Hearing that, Michael began laughing so riotously that he eventually started coughing, and at times it was hard to tell one noise from the other.

Tess stayed right with him, both in mood and by the unwanted complaints from her irritated lungs. Everybody in the city had been affected by the bad air to some degree, even those who had arrived after the fires had been quenched. Such things were to be expected, they'd been told, but that didn't make it easier to tolerate, particularly when it hampered normal activity as well as speech.

Rubbing Michael's back through his cotton shirt to soothe him, she fought her own urge to continue coughing. "Are you okay?"

"Sure," he managed. "Just got carried away."

"You shouldn't laugh at poor Phineas," Tess said, smiling. "After all, he's probably going to spend the rest of his life in jail." The smile widened. "While you get to spend yours with me."

"Well…"

She gave him a playful punch on the shoulder and saw him break into the endearing Irish grin she had always loved seeing. Then he enfolded her in his embrace once again and Tess knew all was right with her little corner of the world.

* * *

Michael watched Gerald Clark start to march Phineas toward one of the guardhouses that had been set up to help maintain order in the refugee camp. There weren't many soldiers stationed there, nor were there a lot of police on duty inside the park. Some of their officers had been killed by falling bricks and the able-bodied remaining ones were needed far more to patrol the streets. Looting was still going on, although not nearly as much as it had been several days ago. Even the criminal element seemed cowed by the disaster, as well they should have been.

Keeping Tess close by his side as they walked, Michael and she followed her father. They could hear Phineas whining and begging for Gerald's mercy but judging by the older man's stiff stature and apparently unsympathetic attitude, his former vice president was wasting his breath.

"What do you think will really happen to Phineas? I mean, what if he gives all the money back?" Tess asked Michael.

"Why? Are you plannin' on waitin' for him to get out of prison instead of marrying me, darlin'?"

"Not on your life, mister. I already told you. You're stuck with me."

"Good. Then why worry about anybody else?"

"Because I feel sort of responsible," she said. "I was the one who rejected Phineas. I wonder if he would have stepped outside the law if that hadn't happened?"

"The best way to tell the good people from the bad is

to offer an easy opportunity to do wrong and see what happens," Michael told her. "God does that all the time, especially when He gives us the choice whether or not to believe in Him."

"I suppose you're right."

"You only *suppose?*" He gave her a quick squeeze. "Don't you know that the husband is always right and the wife is duty-bound to abide by his every decision?"

"Oh? Where does it say that?"

He considered telling her he'd read it in the Bible, then thought better of it. Tess was an extraordinary woman, his mental equal without question, and no easy argument was going to influence her much. Living the rest of his life with her was going to be a true adventure, whether she continued to participate in woman suffrage or not.

Purposely changing the subject to reflect his thoughts, he asked, "So, are you planning to settle down and be a normal married woman soon or do you intend to continue dragging my mother to emancipation lectures with you till you're both impossible to live with?"

"I'm already impossible if you ask Papa," Tess quipped. "Besides, I don't know how long it will be before there's even a decent place to hold our meetings. According to rumor, the pavilion burned down."

"Aye. It did."

"See? That gives you a reprieve, at least until some of San Francisco is rebuilt. Papa is already planning to replace his bank right where it used to be."

"Good. I understand a lot of folks are already drawing up plans for bigger and better buildings. I just hope they follow the rules and use steel the way some of the newer places did."

"That didn't help the city hall."

Michael disagreed. "It did as far as loss of life was concerned. The masonry fell but the dome is still standing. They were able to operate a temporary hospital in the basement, too, until the fire got too close and they had to move over here."

Eyeing her father, Michael asked, "How is he doing, anyway? His cough sounds terrible."

"So does yours," Tess replied. "I think he's getting better, though, as long as he takes it easy. Running to get to me is what set him off this time."

"How does he feel about your suffragette interest?"

Laughing, Tess gave Michael a hug as they paused and watched Gerald Clark usher his prisoner into the guardhouse and close the door behind them.

"He hates the whole idea," she said. "The funniest thing is how Rose Dugan keeps trying to convince him he should change his mind and throw his support behind the movement. So does your mother, only she does it from a distance."

Michael arched an eyebrow. "Are you saying what I think you're saying? Has Rose set her cap for him?"

"Sure looks like it to me. Time will tell. They're both lonely and homeless so that puts them on a more equal plane than ever before." She giggled behind her fingertips. "You should see them together. It's really sweet."

"*Sweet* will be when you and I are wed," Michael reminded her. "I have no idea where we'll live or how

I'll support you and my mother both, but I'll manage somehow."

"You'd better," Tess gibed. "Not only am I stubborn, I can be very impatient."

"Are there any more of your sterling qualities you think I should know about?"

"If there were, I doubt I'd tell you," Tess said. She cuddled closer and Michael wrapped her in his embrace.

"Are you ready to give another laudable performance for the spectators?" he asked, speaking more quietly and using one hand to cradle her cheek and tilt her face up.

"I thought you'd never ask," Tess said.

As Michael began to kiss her he was so happy, so sure that theirs was the right match he could barely keep from shouting for joy. Tess Clark was going to become his wife. The details of their life together would fall into place later, perhaps after the city was back on its feet. Whatever trials lay ahead he knew they could face and conquer them as long as they had each other.

He sensed Tess's willingness and deepened their kiss. Knowing that she was eager in spite of the fact that her father might open the guardhouse door and accost them at any moment gave Michael intense reassurance.

Truthfully he was glad his future bride was as hardheaded as she was or she might have listened to her father and married the wrong man just to please her family. Now, that would never happen.

Tess was his.

And he was most definitely all hers.

Epilogue

Tess smiled wistfully as she stood next to the small paddock behind her modest new San Francisco home and watched her mare pace. The horse was clearly approaching the time when she would foal.

One of Tess's hands rested on the top rail of the fence, the other on her own expanded waistline. She briefly closed her eyes and tilted her face up. It felt wonderful to bask in the warmth of the early June sun after so many prior days of fog.

The mare snorted and stamped her feet, restless and demanding attention. Tess put out her hand to stroke the horse's velvety nose. She knew exactly how the poor thing felt, at least she thought she did.

Giving birth was going to be a new experience for them both and one that she, at least, was looking forward to, particularly since her experience helping care for the three darling orphans they'd rescued after the quake. Thankfully all of them had been adopted by their distant relatives just as she'd hoped, and Rachel had even written a few times to tell Tess how happy she and David were with their new family.

Tess sensed rather than heard her husband's approach, looked over her shoulder and smiled. The moment Michael put his arms around her she leaned back, sighed with contentment and gladly let him help support her.

"How are you feeling today?" he asked tenderly.

Tess smiled. "Wonderful, if you like fat women."

"I love this one," he said, kissing her hair.

"I think the mare is close to foaling."

"Are you two having a race?"

Laughing softly, Tess said, "Uh-huh. But I'm not sure who's going to win."

"That's partly why I came home early. The chief was more than happy to switch a few schedules when I explained why I needed a little time off."

He began to massage her shoulders the way he often had lately and she felt the tension easing.

"Did you tell him you were afraid I couldn't handle things by myself? Your mother's right there in the house, you know. I could always call her if I needed help."

"Aye, but you probably wouldn't," Michael said knowingly. "And the last thing we need is to have you trying to pull a foal when you should be resting."

"I know. I just thought my being here would help the mare feel better. She and I have a lot in common."

"I'm far more worried about you than I am about her," Michael said.

Turning, Tess wrapped her arms around her husband's waist as best she could and laid her cheek on his chest.

"As your mother would say, 'Don't you be worryin' now. The good Lord's watchin' over us.'"

"I know. I just love you so much I can't help it."

"Good. See that you stay that way." Her tone remained light but her thoughts had sobered. "And thank you again for agreeing to live up here. I know it wasn't easy for you to accept a loan from Papa." She touched the badge pinned to his coat. "I'm so proud that you got your promotion. You deserved it. And now we'll be able to pay him back much faster, too."

Michael nodded agreement. "If he'd insisted we build a mansion the likes of the one where you grew up, I don't think I could have ever gotten used to it. This size house is much more to my liking." He chuckled. "I suspect I'd like it even better if it wasn't built right next door to your father's new place."

"I know what you mean. I was worried about that to begin with, too, but Rose has been keeping him so well occupied he has little time to bother us."

Lifting her face, Tess displayed a satisfied grin and arched her brows, pausing until she was sure Michael had noticed. "I told you they would eventually become a couple. Papa got to know Rose very well when we were all camping in the park. By the time the new houses were finished, there was no way he could have denied that they belonged together, even if he'd wanted to. And she makes a wonderful stepmother. Now Annie and I really *are* sisters."

"I know, I know. That's one more time when you were right. I've already lost count. It sure surprised me when your father and Rose were finally wed, though, especially since she's still so involved with giving women the vote."

"So is Papa. Now. At least in a monetary way. I can't wait till Rose convinces him to march in the streets carrying an emancipation sign!"

"Neither can I." A chuckle rose from deep in Michael's chest. "No doubt Gerald Clark's society friends are in a terrible tizzy over his marriage. And our wedding, too, although we've given everybody a year longer to get used to you being Mrs. Mahoney."

"It still takes me by surprise occasionally," Tess confessed. "Being your wife is such a blessing it's hard for me to believe all my dreams have come true."

Her vision misted with contentment and joy as she caressed her husband's cheek, smiled and asked, "Are you going to kiss me right now, right here, Michael Mahoney, or do you want to go stand in the middle of Golden Gate Park again so we can draw a crowd?"

"Any place is fine with me, darlin'," he drawled, smiling and bending to begin to answer her request.

Tess thoroughly agreed. She closed her eyes. Right there, right now, she had never been happier.

Just then their unborn baby gave her a swift kick in the ribs, bringing a vivid reminder of the way life was finding new meaning since the devastation.

A bright promise awaited her family, her friends and the rebuilt city of San Francisco. She could hardly wait to see the future begin to unfold.

* * * * *

Dear Reader,

I love history, as you can probably tell. Every book I research teaches me new things and opens my eyes to how our current era compares to the past. Some things remain the same. Faith is one of them. Love for a husband or wife is another. Although affection may be expressed differently, commitment remains. So does the need for understanding and acceptance.

In this story, Tess and Michael are forced to search their hearts and admit their feelings because of a disaster. I truly believe, no matter what comes our way, that we can find some good in anything if we trust the Lord and look to His guidance.

I love to hear from readers. The best way to reach me is by email. Val@ValerieHansen.com. Or you can send a letter to Valerie Hansen, P.O. Box 13, Glencoe, AR 72539.

Blessings,

Valerie Hansen

QUESTIONS FOR DISCUSSION

1. Does it seem strange to you to realize what a short time has actually passed since women had to fight for their rights? (In some places they couldn't even own property.)

2. Why was Annie so scared to go with Tess to the meetings? Could it have been because she'd been raised as a servant, or were affluent women just as unsure of themselves?

3. Was Tess an unusual mistress because she treated Annie as an equal? Would you be comfortable ordering someone else to do all the things you now do for yourself?

4. Have you ever experienced an earthquake first-hand? I have! What did you do? Was prayer your first response? Do you think Tess acted sensibly? How about Michael?

5. Did you know, before reading this story, that quakes can move in different directions and also change the type of shaking before they're done? Why was that so important in San Francisco in 1906? Is it still relevant?

6. Might you react in the same way Michael and Tess did if you were faced with the task of reaching out

to fellow human beings? Even though they could do little to ease suffering, were their meager efforts valuable?

7. Is it logical for a disaster to bring out their affection for each other the way it eventually did, or do you think they were too influenced by the intensity of the events?

8. If Tess had not been so headstrong, would she have been safer, or did her self-reliance play a part in her survival?

9. Did you agonize with Michael when he knew he must not leave his post? Do you know that today's firemen sometimes face the same terrible dilemma? I can't imagine how that must hurt a man who is trying to save lives, can you?

10. If Tess had been trapped by the fire inside a building instead of in the yard, do you know what she should have done? (The air is always better near the floor.) Inside, if she had stood up, one breath of that superheated air would have killed her.

11. When Tess and the others are forced to camp in the park, why is there little complaining? Do you suppose it's because everyone is so thankful to be alive? Why should it take a catastrophe to make us aware of the gifts God has given us?

12. The marriage of Tess and Michael clearly went against society's norms. Was that a sign for the

better? Think of how much more this country will have grown to accept differences by the time their children are adults!

HISTORICAL

TITLES AVAILABLE NEXT MONTH

Available March 8, 2011

A GENTLEMAN'S HOMECOMING
Ruth Axtell Morren

PRAIRIE COWBOY
Linda Ford

THE PROPER WIFE
Winnie Griggs

WANTED: A FAMILY
Janet Dean

REQUEST YOUR FREE BOOKS!

2 FREE INSPIRATIONAL NOVELS
PLUS 2
FREE
MYSTERY GIFTS

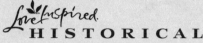

HISTORICAL
INSPIRATIONAL HISTORICAL ROMANCE

YES! Please send me 2 FREE Love Inspired® Historical novels and my 2 FREE mystery gifts (gifts are worth about $10). After receiving them, if I don't wish to receive any more books, I can return the shipping statement marked "cancel". If I don't cancel, I will receive 4 brand-new novels every month and be billed just $4.24 per book in the U.S. or $4.74 per book in Canada. That's a saving of at least 23% off the cover price. It's quite a bargain! Shipping and handling is just 50¢ per book in the U.S. and 75¢ per book in Canada.* I understand that accepting the 2 free books and gifts places me under no obligation to buy anything. I can always return a shipment and cancel at any time. Even if I never buy another book, the two free books and gifts are mine to keep forever.

102/302 IDN FDCH

Name	(PLEASE PRINT)

Address	Apt. #

City	State/Prov.	Zip/Postal Code

Signature (if under 18, a parent or guardian must sign)

Mail to the **Reader Service:**
IN U.S.A.: P.O. Box 1867, Buffalo, NY 14240-1867
IN CANADA: P.O. Box 609, Fort Erie, Ontario L2A 5X3

Not valid for current subscribers to Love Inspired Historical books.

Want to try two free books from another series?
Call 1-800-873-8635 or visit www.ReaderService.com.

* Terms and prices subject to change without notice. Prices do not include applicable taxes. Sales tax applicable in N.Y. Canadian residents will be charged applicable taxes. Offer not valid in Quebec. This offer is limited to one order per household. All orders subject to credit approval. Credit or debit balances in a customer's account(s) may be offset by any other outstanding balance owed by or to the customer. Please allow 4 to 6 weeks for delivery. Offer available while quantities last.

Your Privacy—The Reader Service is committed to protecting your privacy. Our Privacy Policy is available online at www.ReaderService.com or upon request from the Reader Service.

We make a portion of our mailing list available to reputable third parties that offer products we believe may interest you. If you prefer that we not exchange your name with third parties, or if you wish to clarify or modify your communication preferences, please visit us at www.ReaderService.com/consumerchoice or write to us at Reader Service Preference Service, P.O. Box 9062, Buffalo, NY 14269. Include your complete name and address.

LIH11

Love Inspired

With his Dreams Come True foundation, Ethan Fox turns wishes into reality. Now Ethan has come to care deeply for a sick boy whose dream is to have Ethan as a dad. After spending time with the sweet boy and his lovely mother, Lexie Carlson, Ethan wonders if this little boy's wish could come true after all.

A Dad of His Own
by
Gail Gaymer Martin

Available March 2011.

Dreams come True

www.SteepleHill.com

Steeple Hill®

LI87657